CRAZY KILLER!

Pendle's eyes held that milky look of killing madness. He might easily crush Doyle's skull through with the butt and not give a damn . . .

Doyle kicked out, suddenly, with all the strength he could find. A great gasp of explosive effort burst past his lips. He kicked Arthur Pendle just as the killer swung the gun down and Pendle went toppling over off balance. His head crunched into the leg of the table. The gun flew up in the air and curved away to crash down with a heavy thud on the carpet beyond the table.

Doyle took a whooping breath and rolled himself as fast as he could through the door into the kitchen. He kicked the door shut after him on the sight of Pendle wriggling around like a worm on the hook. Doyle had a few moments, a few moments only . . .

Also by Ken Blake in Sphere Books:

THE PROFESSIONALS:
Blind Run

Ken Blake

Based on the original screenplays by
Ranald Graham, Michael Armstrong
(story by Jeremy Burnham), and
Brian Clemens

SPHERE BOOKS LIMITED
30/32 Gray's Inn Road, London WC1X 8JL

First published by Sphere Books Ltd 1979
Novelization copyright © Sphere Books 1979

Set in Intertype Baskerville

Printed in Great Britain by
Hunt Barnard Printing Ltd,
Aylesbury, Bucks.

Chapter One

George Cowley, head of CI5, kept himself fit – and he liked to know his men kept fit, too. The Big A handled assignments too tough for the ordinary run of law-enforcement officers who were hamstrung by rules and regulations. The image built up by CI5 now demanded miracles from the agents, and the men therefore had to handle themselves with just that much extra edge.

So George Cowley, driving to the training area, looked out of the Rover's window and frowned.

Ray Doyle was pounding his feet into the track well enough, flogging along, probably completing his five-mile run. His round cheerful face with the mop of tousled curly hair shone with effort.

But Bodie . . . Bodie drew all Cowley's attention. The chief's lined face expressed total disbelief. He did not run a hand through his thinning sandy hair – maybe that was the way it had become thin – but he was perplexed as he stepped out of the car and confronted Bodie. Doyle panted up and mopped his face with the towel he had flung around his neck.

Bodie stood braced, upright, head flung back. But his hands . . . Bodie's hands were pressed together, palm straining against palm, held over his head. As Cowley and

Doyle watched, fascinated, Bodie's deep rhythmical breathing seemed to drive his hands upwards, pressed together, forming an upward pointing wedge. Up and up those hands struggled like two soaring birds shackled by invisible weights. Slowly they crept up, quivering. High Bodie's hands raked and, quivering, separated as though he was trying to reach into the very heavens. His hands and wrists and forearms shook with his inward effort.

A faint croaking sounded deep in his throat as though torn from him. The groan quickened and deepened and then, his head and hands towering towards infinity, became a roaring burst of sheer sound.

The crescendo was brief. Bodie's hands and arms slumped limply, his head drooped, his whole body sank and softened and he seemed to shrink down to a crouch on the grass. He was, for a moment, blanked out, exhausted by the effort.

Cowley blinked. 'What on earth was that?'

Doyle nodded. 'The sun exercise.'

'The sun!'

Lifting his head slowly and looking up, his lips crinkled in that Bodie-way of wry humour, he spoke with the effort still husking his voice. 'It's Japanese. I'll teach it to you sometime.' His smile grew reflective. 'Not as easy as it looks.'

'I hope,' Cowley said with some acerbity, 'it's made you fit.'

'We're fitter than we've ever been,' protested Doyle, still flushed, mopping with the towel. 'And you know it.'

'But when are we going to know why?' demanded Bodie.

'Tomorrow.'

Bodie and Doyle felt the quick shock of imminent action, a familiar little jolt of excitement. Bodie stood up. Both men were eager, sharpened to a pitch, itching to go. They continued to limber up their muscles, too fit to keep still.

Cowley went on and now he spoke gravely: 'At five a.m. you'll be at St Katharine's Dock with a car on the north quay. A limousine will be there driven by Charlie.' They

6

nodded at this, for Charlie was an agent with whom they had worked before. 'You will wait for a person who will arrive by launch. He is travelling incognito with a bodyguard. He will transfer to the limousine. You will escort him to two addresses, then back to the dock, where the launch will be waiting for him.' Cowley paused, then: 'That's it.'

'That's it?' Doyle's open face registered outrage.

'If,' Cowley said, 'certain people hear of this man's visit to this country – or have already heard of it – there *may* be an attempt to assassinate him.'

'*May?*' said Bodie.

'This man *must* make those two rendezvous, *and* get back to the launch. If you have any – problems – you're freelancers. Neither I nor CI5 exists.'

A tiny pause hung. Bodie and Doyle exchanged a look which said, now what's the old man up to?

Abruptly, Cowley stuck out his hand. Disbelieving, Bodie shook and then Doyle, shaking hands with a faintly ridiculous formality with the chief. Cowley nodded curtly, like a man as satisfied as he can be and yet remaining still dissatisfied, and walked away back to his Rover. Bodie shook his head, staring at the hand just shaken by George Cowley.

'He shook our hands!'

Doyle spoke with a twinkle. 'How could he have – he doesn't exist!'

Once, this dock had taken in the shipping of the world. The warehouses had opened their capacious interiors to the merchandise that would have made the Queen of Sheba green with envy. Tall masts once festooned the sky with spiderwebs of rigging. Now the tall grey warehouses frowned down emptily and the water lapped idly against the worn stones. The large black limousine parked by the steps, looking like a beetle on look-out duty, seemed out of place in the deserted docks. The air of waiting held an exhaustion that even a few inquisitive pigeons could not dispel.

Suddenly with the roar of powerful diesels the deserted dock came to life. A launch splintered the dark water, creaming a white wake in to the stones. Her superstructure, glassed in, the powerful clean lines of her hull, the whipping radio antennae, all jolted a harsh modern note into the crumbling legacy of the dock.

Bodie checked through his binoculars and said: 'This looks like it.'

At his side in the silver-grey Capri they'd picked up from CI5's motor pool, Doyle nodded.

As the launch swung in a wide nicely-calculated arc to sidle up to the quay, Doyle and Bodie got out of their car and walked slowly across to the black limousine. They took up their positions, one at each end of the limousine, and looked around the docks. They methodically held their gaze on the skyline of jumbled roof tops, shadowy corners, the hard angles of windows.

The diesels rumbled into reverse, gouting greenish-white water. The launch rocked and a crewman leaped the gap and started up the steps. He wore a dark anonymous sailor's sweater and trousers, an agile man, knowing what he had to do, with the swarthy cast of features of a southern European. With the deftness of the sailor he looped the rope over the old bollard. Down on the launch the cabin door opened.

The man who emerged on to the narrow deck dwarfed everything. He was immense. His dark coat strained over his shoulders, his head hunched down, round and hard like a cannonball. He looked carefully about him before running up the steps like a great cat of the jungle clawing up a tree.

At the top he hesitated, favoured Bodie and Doyle with two hard scrutinising looks that would have melted armour plate. Then, smoothly despite his bulk, he moved to the limousine and knocked on the front window.

Charlie let the window down and the massive bodyguard bent and looked in. Then he opened the rear door and sniffed around in the passenger section. He stepped away from the limousine leaving the rear door wide open. He checked Bodie and Doyle again and then took a long slow look around the entire dock area. About him the sense of massive power in complete calm command, added to that hint of a foreign flavour, made of him a man to whom instant respect would be accorded.

In a clipped and humorous aside, Doyle said: 'I like it!'

Casually adjusting their positions so as to cover the steps up from the launch, the two agents saw the bodyguard looking across at the Capri. The big man tapped Doyle on the shoulder and pointed quizzically towards the car. Bodie smiled. He pointed at the car in turn, then at his chest. The bodyguard nodded, satisfied, and went down the steps without hesitation.

Doyle smiled. 'What'll we call him?'

A number of apposite and impolite names occurred to Bodie.

Doyle went on: 'Tinker Bell.'

Bodie let his mobile lips widen. 'Roger.'

A small figure wearing the type of Arabian headgear often called a *hatta* emerged on to the deck of the launch. He wore a lightweight two-piece grey suit, and the cloth headgear, with its coiled rope around his head, gave him just that touch of exotic foreign charm that made a CI5 agent's hand twitch towards his holstered gun. The *hatta* hid his face except for his eyes. He was escorted up the quayside steps by his huge bodyguard.

The partners intensified their surveillance. They were both aware that at any moment a livid streak of flame and the spiteful crack of a high velocity rifle could waste the little man. This was the kind of assignment where an agent felt like a clay pipe in a shooting gallery. The tension was there, all the time, only sometimes it grew worse and, after that, somehow it never quite relaxed.

The bodyguard escorted the little man in the *hatta* to the bullet-proof limousine and slammed the door.

With that as the signal, Bodie and Doyle felt the tension ease just a trifle. They went across to the driver's window

9

and as it slid down they listened intently.

'Okay,' said Charlie, crisply, trying to make it all sound matter-of-fact, as though he was just a taxi driver picking up a fare. 'Where to?'

The bodyguard's voice came over the car intercom: 'Twenty-two, Alston Avenue, North West Eight.'

'Got it.' Charlie clicked off the intercom. He looked up at the partners, a tough, easy-going young man who had been trained in the same merciless school. 'Know the way?'

'You go first,' Doyle told him. 'To start with. We may change that later.'

Charlie nodded. His voice sank. 'Who *is* that geezer?'

Doyle and Bodie exchanged glances, reading each other's probable thoughts, enjoying that feeling.

Bodie said: 'Peter Pan?'

Relishing the private continuing joke, Doyle said: 'Roger!'

Charlie, looking suitably baffled, started the engine. Moving off to their own car, Bodie and Doyle suddenly stopped. It was Doyle who whipped back and yanked the limousine door open.

Very strictly, he said: 'Uh, huh!'

'I,' Charlie protested with great indignation, 'was just going to lock it.'

Doyle looked at him. Charlie licked his lips. Ray Doyle, for all his round happy face and tousled hair could, when he wished, look as devilish as Bodie.

'Windows, too,' Doyle told Charlie. He slammed the door and walked away. He passed the sailor by the bollard and favoured him with a guarded but friendly smile. The sailor ignored him. Trained, Doyle reflected, trained to do a job – like us.

Bodie eased the Capri forward to follow the limousine as Doyle slouched down into the front passenger seat. The sailor removed the rope and threw it down where it was swiftly hauled in. He took the second rope and jumped aboard the launch. The diesels, which had remained running, revved up. Smoke plumed. Water boiled away from

10

under the fantail and the launch curved away from the dockside. Doyle watched this through the rear windows of the Capri. He frowned.

Abruptly he grabbed the walkie-talkie. His hand clenched. He spoke rapidly but with emphatic diction.

'Wait a minute!'

Bodie slammed on the brakes and the Capri jolted to a nose-down stop.

Doyle rapped into the walkie-talkie. 'Charlie. Hold it!'

Charlie brought the limousine to a slightly more sedate stop. Doyle glared at the launch now speeding away. Then he swivelled to give his partner a meaningful look.

'Why is the launch leaving?'

Both agents looked at the launch, at the limousine, back at the launch with her wake of disturbed water. Finally, leaning back, Bodie said: 'I don't know.' He looked hard at his partner. 'Why *shouldn't* the launch be leaving?'

Doyle's frown lent a most undecided look to his face, as though he suspected a gasleak and had a cold in the head. 'I don't know.'

With his hand poised on the gear lever, Bodie said with heavy emphasis: 'Can we go now?'

Determined to bluff his way out of this situation, where tension had led him to overcaution, Doyle patted Bodie's hand. 'Yes, James. But not too fast.'

Bodie let Doyle see his entire lack of amusement at the byplay and as he started the Capri again, Doyle told Charlie over the walkie-talkie to get going. The two cars rolled out of the docks and threaded their way through the dingy grey streets. The first hurdle had been cleared safely. That little lapse of Doyle's indicated merely the tremendous pressure the agents felt, the sense that something disastrous could happen any second, and, given Cowley's odd behaviour, probably would. Doyle had been ferretting on in his memory about Cowley.

'When was the last time Cowley shook your hand?'

Without hesitation, Bodie said: 'When I signed on.'

'Me, too.'

11

Morosely, Bodie said: 'He's been meeting a lot of foreigners lately. They do it all the time.'

The blaring howl of a car horn dragged their attention away from Cowley's dark designs and back to the business in hand. A brown Granada hurtled up on the outside, skimming past, overtaking in the most dangerous fashion. Other traffic hauled out of the way, horns whining. The Granada switched in front of the Capri, hugging the tail of the limousine. Doyle's instant reflex action was to reach for his shoulder holster with his right hand. The Granada seized the smallest possible chance in the flow of traffic, pulled out and spurted ahead, overtaking the limousine. Bodie craned forward to watch.

'Moron!'

'Has it gone on?' Doyle lifted the walkie-talkie.

'Yes.'

The hand gripping the walkie-talkie relaxed; but only by a trifle. Doyle shifted around in his seat. 'I don't like this,' he said, and Bodie's mobile lips thinned out in agreement. 'Tinker Bell may look like a Bulgarian – but Peter Pan definitely isn't an Arab.'

'No.'

'I think we're better in front.' Doyle lifted the walkie-talkie. The smell of unease tainted the air in the Capri. 'Hello, Charlie . . . We're going to go in front.'

Bodie tooled the Capri smoothly past the limousine and Doyle gave the sleek car a close scrutiny as they passed. The windows were darkened. He could see nothing of the interior.

'Everything okay?' he said into the walkie-talkie.

Charlie's voice said: 'Yeah.'

'How're your passengers?'

'Quiet as mice. Not a squeak.'

The Capri and the limousine headed north-west through London's traffic, casually speeding up and as casually slowing so that they could remain together as though chained by invisible bonds. The driving skill was neat and unobtrusive. The partners, as usual, were trying to gain a rise out of each other, swopping unlikely stories of their colourful pasts. In Bodie's case the colourful past including exploits like jumping ship and serving as a mercenary in Africa, jumping from aeroplanes as a Red Beret, jumping all over the ungodly, and generally keeping one jump ahead. Then he'd joined CI5 and his life had been all go from then on. Ray Doyle often spun wild stories of a fictitious past to annoy Bodie. He had been a policeman and a detective and the finest pistol shot in the Met. The two worked hand in glove; only they'd never agree who was the hand and who the glove.

Bodie was slyly digging at Doyle with a yarn about that air hostess and Doyle, all agog, said, 'And then?'

'Oh, I didn't tell her I was an airline pilot – I just said I was a pilot. Which is true –'

Doyle interrupted, quietly. 'I think we've got company.'

He checked again, studying the car he felt confident was following them with intent and not merely happening to be going in the same direction. He radioed Charlie, warning him, and with Bodie's consent – Bodie was, after all, driving – told Charlie to stay with them. Bodie swung the Capri sharp left-handed into a street of small London shops alive with the quick trafficking of housewives and children yelling and vans and motor cycles. The limousine followed.

The following car, a brown Triumph, turned left-handed and fell in to the rear.

Three turns later and there was no doubt the Triumph was following them.

Doyle checked with Charlie, who told him there were four men in the Triumph. 'Okay, Charlie. We'll just take it nice and easy.'

'The way I like it.' Charlie's voice on the walkie-talkie brought a quick flash of humour into the situation.

'Well?' Bodie tooled the Capri along.

'We could send Charlie in front?'

Bodie glanced swiftly to his right. 'If they stay too close behind Charlie – *my* seat might get a little warm.'

13

'*And* they might get between us.'

The little procession drove along the road, heading out towards wider streets with less clutter, and as the last car passed a turning, the procession gained an extra member. A dark blue Cortina surged out and fell in on the rear of the Triumph.

Doyle spoke into the walkie-talkie.

'We'll slow down here, give them a chance to overtake.'

Bodie slowed the Capri, and Charlie, mimicking the movement, suddenly shouted over the R/T: 'He doesn't want to know – and there's another one behind him. He doesn't want to overtake, either.'

The partners looked swiftly at each other.

'Shall we take another detour?' Bodie felt those two following cars like leeches hanging on to his backside.

Doyle checked the road ahead and frowned. 'From here there's only one way to that address.' Into the walkie-talkie he said, with a firm bite in his voice: 'Charlie – we're staying to the route.'

The R/T squawked and then Charlie's voice said: 'Anything you say.'

The lights in the surveillance room were dimmed so that the room seemed to float in a muted blue haze. Banks of TV monitors lined the wall. The suggestion of people moving with purpose, and of other people with their attention focused on the screens, added up to an impression of heightened awareness. What was going on outside was reported back on the TV screens, and the men in the room watched, fascinated.

One screen showed with perfect clarity a procession of four cars driving towards a road complex ahead. The Capri, the limousine, the Triumph and the Cortina passed the watchful eye of the TV camera. With the flick of the switch the engineer switched cameras, and now the screen showed the four cars speeding away.

The tension in the surveillance room matched the tension in the Capri as Doyle burst out: 'How far have we got?'

14

Bodie said: 'Bloody miles yet.'

The walkie-talkie squeaked with Charlie's voice: 'Hello, Ray – Tinker Bell's just been on to me. I think he's beginning to panic.'

'What does he want?'

'Keeps yelling at me to go faster.'

Maintaining the same speed, Bodie said: 'Tell him we've got speed limits in this country.'

'We've two alternatives.' Doyle's hand drifted towards his holster again. 'Either we shake them off. Or we don't.'

'Brilliant,' Bodie said. 'And if we don't –'

'They either make a move –'

'Or they don't!'

Doyle sighed. 'And if they don't –'

'They keep following us –'

'Until we reach the address.'

'Where we'll be sitting ducks.'

The prospects ahead did not look cosy.

'How did they pick us up in the first place?' demanded Doyle.

Bodie thought back. 'They weren't at the dock.'

'Where we didn't know our destination.'

'So someone must have told them. Someone at the dock. Or someone on the launch?'

The Capri drove at the same speed and, with that nasty thought about betrayal from the launch that had brought the mysterious personage to the dock, Bodie saw the traffic lights ahead. He changed down, willing the lights to change, willing them to change to red-amber and then green before he reached the crossroads. He addressed the lights as though they were recalcitrant recruits.

'Come on! Change . . . Change!'

Just as he was about to slam the anchors on, the lights changed. The few cars ahead started off and Bodie was able to keep the Capri tooling along and pick up speed without stopping. Doyle swallowed. He glanced back.

'All through.'

Both men knew they had to make a decision about

15

moving. The men in the two following cars would make their move soon, and the CI5 agents had to out-think and out-fight them.

'Well?' said Bodie.

As he spoke a car flashed past on the other side of the road. Bodie caught a blurred glimpse of rust-red and then the car swerved wildly in between the back of the Capri and the following limousine. The tyre screech jerked Doyle's head around. Charlie managed to halt the limousine before it collided with the intruding car. All hell broke loose.

Bodie stamped on the brakes. The Capri slewed wildly and Doyle flung open his door and leaped out, his pistol in his fist. The Browning auto snouted at the rust-red car.

Shots cracked wickedly into the morning air.

Bullets spanged off the cars.

Bodie rammed in reverse and the Capri took off backwards with its tyres spinning so fast the rubber smoked. He went careering backwards, past the stalled limousine, and rammed sternfirst into the Triumph. The tortured shriek of metal added to the din of shots. Bodie's instant action had halted the tailing cars, forcing their occupants to dive for cover as, hightailing out of the Capri, Bodie opened fire.

The flat taste of cordite hung on the air.

Doyle, still shooting, reached the limousine.

He wrenched open the passenger door and ducked down as bullets thunked with a metallic spang into the armoured body.

Bodie raced back through a criss-crossing storm of fire, reached the limousine, dived into the passenger seat. Charlie waited no longer. He stamped on the accelerator and the big black car gunned forward.

They went careering along with Doyle hanging on to the open door for dear life with his left hand, and pressing the trigger of the Browning with his right forefinger. He could feel the sweaty butt of the gun slick in his fist. The

16

dark-featured men in the pursuing cars continued shooting as the limousine speeded up.

Charlie swerved the big car up on to the pavement and sliced past the rust-red job, bumped down into the road and opened her up.

Bodie got a grip on Doyle's collar and yanked him in. Charlie was really belting the limousine along. Other cars sped past going in the opposite direction; but the road continued straight for a space before the traffic complex opened out. Everyone could feel the wind blustering into the car and with it the rank smell of impending disaster.

'Keep going!' bellowed Doyle.

He wriggled around and with Bodie's hefty assistance crammed himself into the passenger seat.

The big limousine howled along the road.

Back at the scene of the action the men from the three cars gathered in a gesticulating and angry group. Their over-sharp clothes and pointed shoes confirmed the impression of their dark-featured faces that they were of Middle Eastern origin. Their eyes expressed anger and disbelief. The reflexes of the two English agents had astonished and disconcerted them. After a few moments yelling at one another they piled back into their cars and set off, leaving Bodie's Capri slewed across the road snarling up traffic.

And, all the time, from an inoffensive-looking van parked off the crossroads, a hard-faced man aimed his telephoto camera and clicked stills of the action – and, most particularly, of the Middle Eastern men. The camera shutter went click-clack, rapidly, and the faces went down on film.

The grim determination in those faces to finish the job they had so far bungled promised no good news for the important personage visiting England – or for Doyle and Bodie.

The ritual of checking out any place of assignment had been hammered into the CI5 agents. They knew what had to be done, and until they had done it they wouldn't allow the man in their charge, this Mr X, to enter what might be a lethal trap.

Charlie slowed the limousine and turned gently through rose-red brick pillars where the wrought-iron gates bore the stunted butts of heraldic devices and tooled the black car sedately along the gravelled drive. The tyres made a thick satisfied crunching. A luxurious mansion came into sight beyond a curve where the rhododendron bushes hung thick with glossy dark-green leaves. The mansion was kept up in good style, and the windows shone, the trellises bore tended plants, the paths were swept. There was money here – money and power. The limousine drew to a gentle stop opposite the ornate front door with its plastered pillars.

Doyle and Bodie alighted and, in tantly, continued the surveillance that took in the trees and bushes, the hedges, the corners of the house, the suggestion of garages and vegetable gardens beyond a tall brick wall.

The front door of the house opened. The man who appeared wore sober clothes of Savile Row cut, shoes that shone with a deep lustre, a white shirt and impeccable tie. His hair was expensively dressed. His face bore the hall-marks of competence in his work – and that work was not opening doors and greeting guests.

The partners for the moment ignored him.

Doyle leant into the car and told Charlie: 'All clear.'

Charlie nodded and repeated it into the car intercom.

The immense bodyguard they had nicknamed Tinker Bell emerged. He took his long slow careful look around. Bodie and Doyle allowed him that as they took up their positions, very similar to those they had adopted at the dockside. Presently, when Tinker Bell was happy about the situation, he escorted Mr X, still wearing his concealing *hatta*, towards the front door of the mansion.

Only when the three men had vanished into the interior did Doyle and Bodie follow. They did not turn their backs on that greenery and they moved smoothly and with great economy of effort. They were still only too well aware that there was a fly in this ointment, and that the men who were out to deal with Peter Pan, Mr X, had not finished yet.

The interior of the mansion was even more opulent than the exterior and the ambassador in his Savile Row suit led the way to a room off the main hall. Before he was allowed to enter for the conference with Mr X, Bodie and the bodyguard checked the room very thoroughly.

There were no windows. Bodie clicked his tongue against his teeth at that. On a small inlaid table coffee and cakes had been tastefully set out. The armchairs were deep and comfortable-looking. Satisfied, Bodie went out and the bodyguard took up a sentry position beside the door. Bodie walked slowly along the hall to join Doyle.

Doyle turned. His voice was grim. 'Those guys *must* have known our route in advance.'

'They could have followed us from the docks.'

'They didn't. You know it.'

'If,' suggested Bodie, 'they'd had a series of lookouts?'

'If they knew he was coming off that launch they would have nailed us down at the dock.'

'You're saying it wasn't anyone on the launch who tipped them off?'

They paused and then, simultaneously, looked along the hall at the bodyguard. He stood, broad and bulky, his cannon-ball head thrust down into his shoulders, impassively by the door.

Bodie said on a breath: 'Tinker Bell?'

The bodyguard had been acting like a bodyguard. Well, if he was double-crossing his employers then he would act his part, and act it well. There was no way at the moment of checking on that suspicion, and the intense accuracy with which Tinker Bell followed the formal lines of protection of V.I.P.s had impressed the partners. He was doing a job; let him get on with it until the moment he put a foot wrong. Then . . .

They checked the house out as much to fill in the waiting

time as anything. The ambassador and Mr X were talking and the house remained quiet and empty. Deliberately empty. Bodie went up the curving staircase with the balustrades carved into the exotic shapes of heraldic beasts. The carpet engulfed his feet to the ankles. He looked out of a front upstairs window on to the garden and the trees and over the wall to the leafy road beyond.

A car glided into sight, disappearing beyond trees and then re-appearing to halt at the kerb a few yards from the open front gates. Bodie frowned. The car was a brown Triumph. He could see the dents and batterings in the front.

A second car drove into sight, passed behind the trees, drew quietly to a halt by the kerb. Bodie's face drew down and his eyebrows indicated the dim view he was taking of all this. Whoever was following Mr X had remarkable sources of information. Sources of information that, it was perfectly clear, were denied the CI5 agents.

Pulling back from the window, Bodie made for the landing and the stairs.

His departure from the upper window was duly recorded by the spying eye of the TV camera mounted in one of the trees in the garden. The transmitted image showed up on a TV screen in the dimmed surveillance room where every move made was acutely observed and commented on.

Going down the stairs Bodie saw Doyle with the telephone handset in his hand, his mouth close, speaking in a quiet voice. Instantly, Bodie called out.

'Cut it!'

Doyle pressed the bar down, looking up with a blank face as Bodie came down the remaining stairs.

'Who are you calling?'

Doyle shot a swift glance at the bodyguard, impassive by the conference room door, and said: 'The Great White Chief.'

'You can forget it. He doesn't exist, remember?'

'Only if we've got problems.'

Bodie waited a moment, a moment which tingled in the

air, then, his wry smile lop-sided, he told Doyle: 'We've got problems.'

Doyle thumped the phone back without another word and the partners went back upstairs. Bodie nodded out of the window and now it was Doyle's turn to study the opposition.

There were now three cars out there, and the Middle Eastern men were moving very casually about, fabricating excuses like asking for lights, one from the other, so as to mask their intense interest in the mansion behind the walls and gate. Doyle saw at a glance that the cars were now positioned so as to be in the best place to ambush any car leaving the gates. Over his shoulder, Bodie took it all in.

'They're going to block us off as soon as they see us coming. They've got all the time in the world.'

'What about the back?'

'I've checked.' Bodie shook his head. 'No way.'

The sound of voices raised loudly in the hall brought Doyle and Bodie running down the thickly-carpeted stairs. The tall ambassador, talking rapidly in a foreign language to Mr X, glanced up as the partners appeared. The feeling of abrupt chill in the air clawed at them. This thing hadn't really started yet, not with a gang of murderous cut throats outside ready to ram and shoot them to Kingdom Come.

The ambassador made a small gesture to Mr X.

'He is ready to leave.' He handed a slip of paper across and Doyle took it. 'I have here the next address he has to be taken to.' Then he went back to speaking rapidly to Mr X. Peter Pan remained muffled in his cloth headgear.

Doyle pulled Bodie aside. The partners had to make a decision, they had to make the right decision, and they had to make the right decision work.

'There's only one thing we can do,' said Doyle, forcefully.

The foreign language broke off and the Ambassador spoke impatiently in English.

'Excuse me. He is in a great hurry.'

Doyle, holding down his own impatience, snapped out: 'Does he want to get there alive?'

This shook the ambassador. He blinked. Peter Pan rattled off a quick comment or query and the bodyguard rolled to the window in the hall alongside the door. He peered out like the inhabitant of Notre Dame looking down on the mob. He swung that cannon-ball head around and looked calmly at the partners.

'We go.'

Bodie said with a crispness that Doyle, for one, relished: 'We give the orders around here, Tinker Bell. You do as we say.'

Doyle took out his walkie-talkie.

'Hello. Charlie?'

The R/T squeaked back. 'Charlie here.'

'Listen carefully,' said Doyle, and he gave Bodie a meaningful look. Bodie went off to the kitchen in search of what was required as Doyle told Charlie what he had to do.

Outside in the street the opposition watched all movement carefully. So did the spying eyes of the TV cameras in the tree.

A small man wearing a cloth *hatta*, the rope slipping a little, was escorted out and into the limousine. The would-be assassins moved gently to their cars and the engines started. Blue exhaust smoke plumed on the air.

Bodie settled at the wheel of the armoured limousine. He engaged 'drive' and opened the throttle and the big car eased forward, tyres scrunching fatly on the gravel.

At that precise moment outside the kitchen quarters of the mansion, beyond the rose-red brick wall, Doyle sat at the wheel of a Ford Fiesta. The bodyguard sat with him. Both men felt the tension mount as the soft purr of the limousine engine and that crunching gravel told them the time to leave had arrived. That was the part of it all that amused as well as appalled Ray Doyle. You started off and left, and the next minute you were in it up to your neck.

This time it was down to Bodie ...

The limousine ground forward heading for the open gates.

The dark blue Cortina edged into view, aiming to block the exit.

Bodie slammed his foot on the accelerator pedal.

The big car smashed forward. Bodie's gun hand jammed on the horn button and the horn screeched like a banshee. Gravel spat away from the tyres. The crash lights blinked on and off. Headlong the limousine hurtled towards the gates and the Cortina.

Guns spat fire. Bullets spanged off the armoured limousine. Driving with an exact skill Bodie held the bonnet of the car straight on the Cortina, hit it smack on, sending it lurching aside. Bullets caromed and whined and cracked. Straight for the gap charged Bodie, wreathed in smoke and dust and flying gravel, the lights flaring and the horn wailing, shrouded in a storm of gunfire.

Chapter Two

In the surveillance room that wild charge of Bodie's brought startled exclamations to the lips of the observers. In the dim lighting they studied with avaricious eyes the way the big limousine smashed out, knocking the Cortina aside, hared on with the bullets bouncing off it like peas off a drum. The observers saw the assassins racing for their own cars and beginning the next stages of the chase.

Despite the damage sustained by the Triumph in its argument with Bodie's Capri, and now the Cortina in its confrontation with the armoured limousine, both cars would still run. They revved up and hared off in pursuit.

Then more gasps escaped the observers in the surveillance room as a Ford Fiesta trundled sedately out past the gates and turned to drive on after the chase.

At a crisp order the recorded videopictures were re-run. This time the observers concentrated on the men involved in the attempt on Mr X.

One jabbed a stiff forefinger at the screen, indicating a swarthy man shooting fast and accurately at the limousine as it bundled past. In a thick foreign accent he called out excitedly: 'It's him. It's Ramos!'

Other voices took up the task of identification.

'That one there – it could be Sylvan.'

Again the video recording was run. The dim surveillance room echoed to excited sounds of recognition.

In the Fiesta Doyle drove fast but carefully. He took a quick peep over the back seat.

Curled up on the floor with his hands over his face, Mr X, still wearing his *hatta*, looked the picture of frightened innocence. Doyle made a face and went back to driving. He yanked out his walkie-talkie and spoke viciously.

'This is Doyle calling Bodie. Doyle calling Bodie. Can you hear me?'

But the only answer was the ominous and empty hiss of the walkie-talkie on full volume.

The limousine, in startling contrast to the easy pace of Doyle's Fiesta, was belting along, hurtling around corners with tyres screeching, lurching right over on the springs.

Bodie glanced into the mirror. Charlie was kneeling on the back seat looking out. The makeshift *hatta* and chunk of rope lay discarded at his side.

Charlie let out a yell.

'Here they come.' Two cars sped into view as the limousine swung along a straight street, the houses passing in a blur beyond their screen of trees. The day was still young, and yet villainy had been stalking abroad for some time and was now in full cry astern. Charlie looked disgusted.

Bullets smashed into the back of the limousine. The rear window abruptly starred and turned opaque, like curdled milk.

'They're shooting at us!' said Charlie, indignant at the very idea.

There were only two cars following now. Evidently the dark blue Cortina had given up the ghost at last, ruptured by the armoured limousine's bull-like charge. But all the men were crammed into the remaining two cars, and they were hotly pursuing; as the bullets thwacked and cracked into the limousine, it was clear they meant business.

Charlie leaned in through the opened partition and took up Bodie's walkie-talkie. He spoke crisply.

'Hello, Ray. Can you hear me? This is Charlie calling.'

The only answer he got was the loud spang and spatter of bullets hitting the bodywork of the limousine.

The silence of the radio worried Ray Doyle. He drove at a more sedate speed, trundling through a suburban street. The bodyguard turned away from the back window, at last satisfied, and said something in their common language to Mr X. Doyle's lips crinkled up.

'Share the joke, Tinker Bell,' he said, grittily.

'It has worked.' The bodyguard sounded as pleased as though he'd figured it all himself in that round head of his. 'They have lost us.'

Under his breath, Ray Doyle said: 'I'm not worried about you two fairies. It's just my job.' He half-tilted his head back, still concentrating on the road ahead. 'Is he a nice chap, your friend? We're all risking our lives for him. I hope he's worth it.'

For Ray Doyle that was a remarkable admission of the state he was in. He spoke again, savagely, shouting into the walkie-talkie.

'Doyle calling Bodie! Can you hear me? We are okay. Proceeding as planned. Can you hear me?'

Only that mocking frying-pan hiss spat nastily up from the walkie-talkie.

Bodie was belting the big limousine along at a very fast clip, a very fast clip indeed, and his R/T was of no use to him just at that moment. Charlie wetted his lips in the back and ventured some advice.

'Jam the brakes on. The back can take it.'

Bodie considered and rejected the notion in a single flash. Yes, the armoured limousine could stop suddenly and the first pursuing car would make a nasty mess of itself up the tail pipe. But – 'We've got to give Doyle all the time we can.' He kept his foot planted firmly on the accelerator, looking as far down the road as he could, seeing the roundabout sign whirling up towards him. 'Are they both still there?'

Charlie opened his mouth to answer and a bullet cracked viciously into the glass before his face. It did not penetrate; but Charlie jerked back as though a wasp had landed on his lip. 'Yes!'

'Okay. Hang on tight!'

Bodie hit the roundabout something like fifteen miles an hour too fast. The limousine leaned right over, groaning, as he flailed the wheel around. The tyres skidded, screeched and bit. The car lurched around and straightened up before Bodie swung the wheel the other way fairly hurtling the big limousine around the roundabout. The two other cars followed, their tyres shrieking like rusty sheaves.

Around Bodie went, leaning against the centrifugal force, belting the limousine around so that suddenly he was on the tail of the second car. Around and around they went. It was, if your humour was macabre enough, rather comical.

Charlie was hopping about in the back trying to see ahead.

The first car, the Triumph, hauled off to the side and halted at the kerb, the front near-side tyre hitting the granite hard. The second car and the limousine in pursuit went belting past. Bodie gave the halted Triumph a nasty look as he whirled past.

At the next turn-off, with a dextrous turn of the wheel, he sent the limousine spinning off and slewed her hard into a one-eighty degree turn, the brakes locked on and tyres smoking. The limousine spun around and as Bodie thumped back on the accelerator again hared back into the roundabout going the wrong way.

Two men had climbed out of the Triumph and had unlimbered their artillery. They were lining up on the limousine when the big car smashed straight for them. Bodie knew exactly what he was doing. The gunmen in front, poised in the stance, their guns aimed in clenched fists, suddenly realised what was happening.

In the next second the limousine would roll right over them like a Juggernaut.

That, considered Bodie with a juicy smile, would be all right with him.

The gunmen leaped for safety, coat tails flying, just making it to the kerb. Bodie flicked the wheel and tooled the limousine past the Triumph. Those would-be assassins had no time to shoot.

On he went, around the roundabout the wrong way, and, surprise, surprise! Here came the second car, charging along all agog to get some action.

Bodie's mobile lips thinned. He bent a little. He set the limousine straight and fairly hurled the armoured monster at the car. He felt like an S.E.5a pilot with hammering Vickers charging straight for a Fokker D.VII with Spandaus licking vivid tongues of flame.

Charging head to head – the nerves of the car driver broke. With a savage lurch and the scream of tyres the car hauled out of the way.

Clean through the empty space where the car would have been drove the triumphant Bodie.

He whipped out of the roundabout at the correct turn and was a quarter of a mile along the road before the Middle Eastern assassins gathered themselves together and set off after him.

But Bodie hadn't finished with the opposition yet. He knew the whereabouts of the nearest local police station. The stone-faced brick building came into sight, solid and dependable, the blue lamp long since gone. People stood back from the kerb as the large and opulent limousine with the dents and scratches disfiguring the lovingly-polished body eased into the kerb. A policeman walked up the steps into the station. A taxi appeared with its light shining orange.

Bodie leaped out of the limousine and ran across the road hailing the taxi.

Charlie got out of the car and, with great ostentation, held open the rear door and then stood waiting as though for his passenger. He waited a moment until he saw Bodie safely installed in the taxi which whipped away smartly, and then he walked sedately up the steps and into the police station.

The Middle Eastern gunmen walked cautiously forward to the abandoned limousine. Their guns were hidden; but their gun hands quivered expectantly. They looked in. Puzzled, they started in slanging each other again before, with much recrimination, they hurried back to their cars.

The taxi was gone from their sight, vanished into the London traffic.

Bodie spoke into his walkie-talkie. He spoke with urgency, yet his voice was as icily detached as his brain.

'This is Bodie calling. C5 One. We have an emergency and I am reporting back to base.'

Then he leant forward and gave the off-Whitehall address that was as near as he'd be dropped to CI5 H.Q.

The building to which Doyle drove the Fiesta backed on to the canal. Mainly deserted now, glinting in coloured swirls of oil upon the water, the canal was kept as clean and tidy as the limited funds of the Inland Waterways would allow. Pleasure cruisers and narrow boats used the cut. The serenity of calm water extended its never-failing welcome; but that serenity was brutally chopped-off by the grimed brick walls fringing the cut.

The mansion, too, was hemmed in by brick walls and the leafy trees bowered the building and prevented easy observation. Doyle got out of the car and with a habitual and thorough look around crossed to the iron gates. They were closed. He pressed the button of the intercom set in the gatepost and when it hissed back at him, spoke clearly.

'Escorts Unlimited. We have a visitor for you.'

A click sounded. The gates opened, silently, their electric motors marvels of discreet service. Doyle returned to the car and drove it in past the opened gates.

The house presented itself as, if not quite the counterpart to the ambassadorial residence they had already visited, a very close copy indeed. There was the same discreet air of luxury and power. Doyle carried out the usual checks, and Tinker Bell would not be satisfied until he had also checked the surroundings.

Then, when all seemed well, Mr X was assisted out of the Fiesta and up the steps into the house.

The second ambassador wore as beautiful a suit as the first. After all, any man living in England with money to spend provided by a government anxious to appear of some importance would buy English clothes. But his face had that craggy and yet bulbous look of the Eastern European. His jaw would have served admirably as the ram of a battleship.

The official with him looked not so much a pale imitation of his master as a man with the appearance of a clerkly official and the function of the bodyguard, Tinker Bell. They all went through the hall, furnished in impeccable if lack-lustre taste, and the door of the conference room was thrown open.

Doyle at once moved forward to check the room out.

The official barred his way. His grey suit was most ill-cut about the left armpit. He said something in a torrent of gutturals that Doyle took to mean he couldn't go into the room.

'Do you mind –'

The ambassador said: 'Please –'

The official and the ambassador began a rapid gabbling which Doyle picked up as an argument.

'Listen, you two –' he started.

The sound of a door opening made him automatically check that out. He stopped talking. The woman who walked into the hall was beautiful. Her bone-structure would never fail her. Her skin bore a smoothness and silkiness that might fade; but she would never be less than beautiful. Her eyes regarded Doyle as the bodyguard moved instinctively to shield Mr X. Doyle felt himself impaled on those large brown eyes. He looked. She looked. For an instant, a single betraying instant, Ray Doyle ceased to be

30

a dedicated CI5 agent. For just that single heartbeat he was a man confronted by breathtaking beauty.

And, the attraction was mutual. The woman put a hand to her throat. A ring glittered. She wore simple elegant clothes of a pleasant neutral hue and she looked just right.

She was in her late twenties, and she moved with a lithe and supple grace that made Doyle's back snap up straighter.

The moment the girl appeared the official broke into a torrent of words, glancing at Mr X, glancing at the girl, shaking his head, his thick body tensed with frustration and anger. The ambassador attempted to smooth him down. The woman smiled at Doyle and, although he thought of the smile as pleasant, he knew with a warming glow that it was much more than that.

'What is the problem?'

'Tell them,' said Doyle. 'I just want to check out the room.'

She spoke with a happy-sounding voice, and yet, Doyle picked up a little puzzlement in it as she looked at Mr X in his enveloping *hatta*. The ambassador smiled and said something to the official that sounded as though he had made his point.

'Please . . . ' he said.

Doyle nodded and went into the room as the official stood aside. Then, feeling the eyes of the world upon him, Doyle halted. He offered his arm to the bodyguard, as though offering to take a partner on to the dance floor.

'Tinker Bell?' he said, letting the hidden feelings spill out in this flim-flammery. 'Shall we?'

As the tough bodyguard blinked, Doyle smiled and strolled off into the room.

He checked the room and then crossed to the windows.

At a lower level jagged rooftops interspersed with flat black roofs led to the drop to the canal. There were many nooks and crannies out there. In one of those slots of darkness out there could be a nutter with an Armalite.

But the canal looked peaceful and serene.

31

Doyle shook his head. He felt the old itch up his spine. He turned back to the room and spoke severely to the bodyguard.

'Well, Tinker Bell. Let me tell you. I don't like it one little bit.'

There was no comfort to be gained from the open look of concern on the bodyguard's face.

In the hall, after the ambassador and Mr X had entered the conference room, Doyle started his prowling scouting of the house. The official at once began to protest, gabbling on in his own tongue. Doyle glanced back at the girl, who was about to translate.

'Listen,' he said. 'Tell Bela Lugosi here he needs subtitles.'

He shouldered on to check out the next room. The girl spoke hesitantly to the official who was, quite clearly, a security man, and when Doyle passed back to the opposite door, the CI5 man halted and swept his hand across the space in front of the official's waist.

'Across here – see – in clear white letters, so that when you talk like that, we can read what you're saying.'

The woman started to smile in amused understanding, caught herself, and set those beautiful features into their charming lines of serenity as Doyle prowled off. He was aware of her at his shoulder. He could not fail to be aware of her. She exuded the kind of female attraction he could never resist. He flung open a door and a startled telephone girl looked up, her switchboard quiet. She was quite pretty.

Feeling devilish, Doyle said to the woman: 'You've got competition.'

The remark died as, turning back, Doyle saw the security official looking nervously at his wristwatch. When the security man became aware of Doyle's regard, he looked guilty. The byplay served only to strengthen Doyle's uneasy awareness that wheels were turning within wheels. He felt naked and vulnerable. The switchboard girl looked at him, puzzled, and Doyle managed to scrape up a smile and go off to check the upper floors of the house.

When the cars rolled up to a stop outside the high wall of the house backing on to the canal the TV cameras picked them out mercilessly. Their images were relayed to the screens in the dimly-lit surveillance room. A monitor screen showed a camera picture which zoomed in on the man who was, without a moment's doubt, the leader.

His hard dark face bore the indrawn hate-fuelled fires of the fanatic. He issued his commands curtly and his men obeyed instantly.

The foreign observers in the surveillance room seemed to huddle together. Their voices broke raggedly.

'Yes, we have him! It's Georgio himself.'

Another observer said in his guttural accent: 'Those others don't look like C.P.I. They're more like S.S.!'

The observers continued to watch their screens. The atmosphere in the surveillance room resembled what must be the atmosphere within the dark inner recesses of a spider's lair as his spun web waits to trap unwary flies.

The high wall surrounding the house which prevented the gunmen from looking in also prevented Doyle from looking out. He went up the stairs followed by the woman whose movements were becoming a distraction. The first floor windows revealed trees; the street was still completely hidden. Doyle with his copper's nose felt almost sure – almost to the point of a racing certainty – that the Middle Eastern assassins were out there.

'I need to go higher,' he said.

She walked up close to him. He could sense her there.

'I must talk to you.' Her whisper carried such urgency that Ray Doyle was taken aback. He looked at her, his blue eyes wide in surprise. She looked intense, frightened, and she glanced back over her shoulder as though expecting the security official to be breathing down her neck.

In confirmation of that thought, she went on in a loud voice, a too loud voice that would carry to the others below: 'And that room there is full of cabinets.'

Her hand closed on Doyle's arm. He felt the electric

shock. She drew him to a smaller room off to the side of the landing.

'Leia?' said Doyle, wondering what the hell this was all about.

She shut the door noiselessly. 'You have to tell me.' Her breast rose and fell and her face, although still beautiful, looked too pinched in for Doyle's comfort. 'That *is* Dr Hanish down there, isn't it?'

Suddenly canny, Doyle said: 'Who?'

'If it is Hanish – they will stop at nothing to kill him.'

'Who the hell are they?'

Leia looked perplexed. Her full lips shone as her teeth bit. Then she burst out: 'But then you can't be working for the British!'

'I,' said Ray Doyle, 'am a male capitalist pig.'

She shook her head waving away the feeble irritation of his light-hearted approach. 'Whoever you are – you *are* trying to save him.'

'I get paid cash on delivery.'

Leia looked full at him as though weighing the inner man against the raffish, casually-clothed, easy-going exterior. 'Why are there only two of you?'

Feeling his own strength ebbing, Doyle said: 'Tinker Bell has the strength of ten men.'

'If they find him the British will do nothing to save him.'

Leia paced away from Doyle and the look of concentration on her face made Doyle's heart skip a beat. Then, suddenly, she looked at him again, and this time the pleading look could not be mistaken.

'The British must *want* him killed! I must help you save him.'

Before Doyle could even begin to unravel the twists and double twists he had got himself into with this girl, footsteps sounded hard on the wooden treads of the stairs outside the edges of the thick carpet. Someone was in the devil of a hurry. Doyle and Leia went to the landing.

The security official with another man of exactly similar

appearance ran up, shouting. Leia listened.

She swung excitedly to Doyle. 'The phones have been cut. We are going to try the transmitter. You will also get a better view from up here.'

That had been the object in coming up here; what Leia was maundering about Doyle would have to figure out. They all ran up the next flight of stairs where the official produced a key to unlock the door concealing the topmost flight of stairs. At the top lay a small transmitter room. The equipment was of innocuous Japanese manufacture, and was, by that token, untraceable. The second official sat before the console and started in feeding power to the circuits.

Doyle crossed to the small angled window and looked out.

He could see down over the trees and at once focused in on the cars parked innocently by the kerb. There were a half dozen or so men down there, moving about. A man was crouching by the boot of one of the cars and the sun glinted suddenly and brightly off the object in his hands. Doyle pulled his head in sharply – very sharply.

From above their heads came the dull sound of a blow, then a crackling spatter of shocks as though something had hit the roof and was falling off. The radio equipment emitted a loud plaintive whistling.

'They got the aerial,' said Doyle. This was looking as though the opposition were one step ahead all the way along the line. They'd followed them, they'd been shaken, and now here they were again . . . And shooting down wireless aerials, too . . .

The officials and Leia started in jabbering, obviously as frightened as they were upset. Doyle hauled out his walkie-talkie, a real baby-brother to the equipment in the transmitter room. But, at the least, his R/T was still working.

'Hello, Doyle here. Peter Pan, Tinker Bell and Wendy having a great time. But wish you were here.' He paused. 'Wherever you are!'

He did not add, as the situation warranted, that the ungodly had cut the phone wires, had shot away the radio aerial, and were now moving in for the kill.

Feeling that, conscious of the beauty of Leia and the fear of the officials, Doyle waited for the answering call from Bodie. The walkie-talkie merely hissed, emptily.

The shabby building just off Whitehall that housed CI5 Headquarters was a rundown and seedy sort of place, a jumble of dusty rooms and corridors. The communications, forensic laboratories and equipment sections, together with the basement garage and workshops, were equipped and staffed to a very high degree. Bodie loped down a musty corridor feeling the blood in his temples, wondering what devil of a scrape Ray Doyle had got himself into, feeling his own intemperate nature boiling up dangerously.

Harry Whitlaw, a CI5 operative who had caught H.Q. duty this month, stood guard outside the door to the top-level security rooms. Bodie reached for the door handle.

'Bodie!' snapped Harry Whitlaw, chunky, fair-haired, quite ready to sock anyone on the jaw who tried to get past him. 'You can't go in there. It's off limits to everybody.'

'It's all right, Harry,' Bodie told him. 'I don't exist!'

With that Bodie brushed passed Harry Whitlaw, shoved the door open, and barged in.

Whitlaw followed, outraged, trying to get a grip on Bodie. Bodie bustled on, through the antechamber and into the security room beyond.

'Don't worry, Harry,' Bodie said, reassuringly, anxious to get on. This was no time to get involved in minor matters.

The room was dimly lit and there were a number of people in there, all speaking at once, or so it seemed to Bodie. He glared around. The monitor screens on the walls glowed. He saw a picture of a big black limousine smashing through the gateway of a mansion and knocking a dark blue Cortina out of the way. Bodie saw that. He saw the other TV screens and what they portrayed. He saw the backs of the observers as they hunched forward, like vultures.

The most interest was being shown in a screen which vividly portrayed a high-walled house, with men gathering outside, and, along the kerb, a parked brown Triumph. Bodie felt his anger throbbing within his temples and bloating his throat so that he wanted to spit.

A shadow moved at his side.

A voice, a familiar, demanding, plummy voice, said: 'Just what the hell are you doing here?'

One of the observers sang out: 'They're going to storm the building!'

Harry Whitlaw, flustered, said: 'I'm sorry, sir, but I thought –'

The shadow at Bodie's side waved Harry Whitlaw away. A firm hard hand gripped Bodie's arm and steered him away from that TV screen where Georgio organised his gunmen to break into the house and kill every living soul within.

'Why, Bodie,' said George Cowley in his grating voice, 'why are you here?'

'There's a whole army out there!' Bodie's voice would have cut armour-plate. 'We need help!'

Cowley said: 'The man you are escorting is an enemy of Britain's allies. We can't be seen to be helping him against them.'

'Then,' challenged Bodie, 'why *are* we helping him?'

'*We* are not. *You* are. *We* don't exist. Remember!'

Bodie closed his eyes. This surveillance room had been tracking him all along. He felt sick. His eyes opened and he stared at the screen. It was quite clear the opposition were about to climb the wall. Bodie swallowed.

'Doyle's in there?'

'Yes.'

One of the foreign observers let out a shout, almost, Bodie thought with sick revulsion, as though he was watching some beastly foreign bloodsport. 'They're going to attack! Now!'

37

Hurriedly, George Cowley returned to the monitor screens and his guests. This was high level stuff and he had to balance it all out so delicately that, if anyone got killed – and that seemed a certainty – Her Majesty's Government and the unmentioned, and unmentionable, secret services, would come out smelling of violets. Georgio had organised the car against the wall. The Middle Eastern gunmen climbed up on to the car roof and began to climb over the wall. This was a full scale invasion of the ambassadorial house.

The stark effrontery of the gunmen's move passed without question. This might be London, but when determined men went into action, they could be up and over a wall in no time, and the car used as a vaulting horse be driven circumspectly away. No passing Bobby would then notice a thing.

Cowley half-turned from the screen. His conscience was as muddy as Hell's sewers.

Bodie turned away.

He barged through a group of observers without politeness, ran from the room. By the way he ran, Cowley knew with instant and intuitive sympathy that Bodie was in agony for the safety of his partner.

Well – that was CI5.

He turned back to the screen.

A TV camera mounted in the fork of a tree in the grounds picked up Georgio and his men.

They dropped to the ground inside the wall. They unlimbered their artillery.

They looked menacing, ungodly, and very very murderous.

Silently, they loped towards the house.

Chapter Three

Bodie had taken a maroon Princess II from the motor pool and he swung the sleek car through the traffic, cutting corners, jumping lights, almost daring the traffic police to make an attempt to stop him. The car hummed beautifully and Bodie dragged out his walkie-talkie and bellowed into it as the Princess sliced up a couple of Minis and a Jag, belting back into the white lines as oncoming traffic slewed and blew indignant horns.

'Bodie to Doyle! Bodie to Doyle!'

The R/T merely sent out its maddening hiss.

'Bodie to Doyle! Bodie to Doyle!'

The R/T went smack on to the luxurious seat and Bodie bent himself to driving like a maniac – like a maniac with perfect control of the car and perfect control of his actions.

Ray Doyle's walkie-talkie was in his pocket and Ray Doyle's gun was in his fist.

It was all a hubbub and a commotion in the hall of the ambassadorial residence as people milled. They had seen the gunmen climbing the wall and Doyle guessed what the next step would be. The security official whom he had never trusted was gesticulating violently and pointing to a heavy door set in an angle under the stairs. Leia looked doubtfully at him and back to Doyle. The ambassador looked undecided – he looked dignified, but he looked undecided, too – and the second official was clearly wetting his pants in fear. Leia had a gun. It looked incongruous – blasphemous – in that smooth pink-nailed hand.

'What are they saying, Leia?'

'They're going down to the cellar – '

At that moment the front door shuddered under a smashing succession of impacts. Wood splinters imploded from the lock. Someone outside had just shot half a clip at the doorlock. Doyle leaped for the front window and, smashing the glass, poked his Browning auto out and let rip with a whole clip in reply.

The security official tried to drag Mr X to the cellar steps, jabbering words that obviously meant that Peter Pan must go down with the others. Mr X, although his features were concealed by the *hatta*, was clearly quaking.

Leia shouted: 'They want him to go down with them!'

Doyle flung a glance at the bodyguard. The scene was slipping away. The door shuddered under fresh impacts. Any minute it would burst open and then the murderous gunfire would cut them all down.

Doyle yelled at the bodyguard.

'No! You stay up here.'

And, to Leia: 'Tell them to do what I say!'

Leia shouted quickly at the ambassador and the security official scowled and would have begun an argument. Doyle let his Browning wave briefly in their general direction. That settled that. More shots slugged into the door. The bodyguard joined Doyle by the window, his own weapon – a fancy version of a Walther – at the ready.

Doyle told him savagely: 'We go down to that cellar, Tinker Bell, and we're trapped for good.'

More shots pelted in through the smashed window and knocked a pair of green Chinese vases to smashed ruin. The security official grabbed the ambassador and fairly ran him to the cellar door. The second official, who was probably just a radio operator, spread his hands helplessly and then scuttled across to join them. They trooped down to the cellar. The cellar door slammed.

'Up,' said Doyle. 'And make it fast!'

They hustled Mr X with them and hared up the stairs.

Doyle crouched on the landing. He reloaded the Browning again, and calculated the remaining stock of rounds he carried. It would be a near thing.

The door was on its last legs. Bullets continued to punch in through the front windows and carome about the hall. Doyle saw the bodyguard hustling Mr X up the next flight of stairs and running to look through the front windows. Mr X stood for a moment, his *hatta* ludicrous, a limp, pathetic, frightened puddle of a man.

Doyle returned his attention to the front door.

'Leia – Go on – *Now!*'

Doyle sent four swift shots through the rapidly widening gap in the door. He looked up. Leia crouched by the banisters on the top landing. He bellowed up to her.

'Now cover me!'

Leia aimed her gun at the door as Doyle legged it up the stairs four at a time. He hit the landing and slid to a halt at Leia's side. Looking through the banisters he saw the shambles of the hall with bullet pocks on the walls and smashed vases and a table riddled through. He crouched by Leia, and held his Browning pointing at the door.

Very quietly, very gravely, he said: 'What was that name again?'

'Leia.'

'Leia. Listen to me carefully. I want to tell you something.'

'Yes?'

'I think I'm in love.'

Her brown eyes regarded him thoughtfully, although what her thoughts were Doyle had no idea. He caught a fleeting memory and hoped she wouldn't say: 'Who are you in love with?' for that would mean she was dense or cruel, and he didn't think she was either. Before she could speak a hurricane of shots burst through the door. The shattered wood went down. A group of men hurled themselves in and dived for cover as Leia and Doyle shot down on to them.

Gunsmoke wreathed flatly. The slugs caromed and spat about the hall and stairs.

'Up, again,' snapped Doyle. 'I'll hold 'em – you get Tinker Bell and Peter Pan away aloft. Sharp, now.'

Leia crawled back into the cover of the landing and then, without a word of protest, ran to do as Doyle bade her.

The maroon Princess screeched around the last corner and Bodie hurled the car into a sliding skid as he jammed on the anchors. He snatched up the R/T and snapped into it with a crackling note of urgency in his voice that he fought to keep under control.

'Hello, Doyle. This is Bodie. I'm right with you!'

The walkie-talkie emitted its infuriating squeaks and hisses and then – then Ray Doyle's voice crackled through.

'Bodie! We're working our way backwards – should be able to make it to the canal.'

Bodie looked back along the street, saw the crossroads, and the Princess seemed to come alive and go screeching backwards in reverse, around the corner, still in reverse, go sliding down to the very lip of the canal. The grimy brick wall parted to either side and the curved arch of the bridge carrying the road allowed a muddy access to the towpath. Bodie slithered down like a wildcat out of a tree.

A row of moored boats looked as though they were all on the point of sinking. At the far end, moored up, lay a spanking cabin cruiser, all fibreglass and gloss and a shiny outboard motor.

Bodie leaped down, clambered on to the nearest boat, began to run and skip and leap his way along to the cabin cruiser.

He was unfastening the moorings from their pins when a woman popped up through the companionway hatch. Her face expressed grave concern for Bodie's sanity. She didn't look in the slightest concerned or frightened. She wore a towelling dressing-gown which emphasised the voluptuous curves of her figure. Her face was carefully made up, quite unnecessarily, for she held an inner beauty that made Bodie look twice.

When she spoke her voice jarred with its lacerating upper-class accent that so irritated Bodie's sensibilities.

'Just,' said this apparition, 'what the bloody hell do you think you are doing?'

'I'll tell you in a minute.'

Bodie leaped for the controls. The outboard had to start first time. He yanked. The engine fired. With a grunt Bodie climbed behind the wheel and opened the throttle. The cabin cruiser curved away from the bank with sundry gratings and bumpings from under the keel. The woman looked as though she could hit Bodie.

'My good man –'

Bodie had no time for that nonsense. He savaged the boat along the canal, already searching the backs of the houses with his intolerant gaze, his hand reaching for the walkie-talkie.

'What are you?' said the woman. But her voice was – small – Bodie felt, not quite ignoring her.

He sighed. 'I'm nothing. I don't exist!'

Then he favoured her with one of those famous Bodie smiles. She swallowed, and backed off into the corner of the cockpit, huddling the towelling dressing gown about herself. Bodie had no time to admire the resultant scenery – Ray Doyle was in trouble. He shoved the throttle full open.

'Is this as fast as it goes?'

The greyish-greenish-whitish wash slopped in a double-arrowed fan out to the banks where the water clucked and splashed and recoiled. Mud roiled up. The damage Bodie was doing would infuriate any intuitively sensitive narrow boat person ...

The woman's lips trembled. 'Who *are* you?'

You had to admit, Bodie considered, the situation was

enough to make anyone nervous, if not downright scared. But needs must ... He smiled pleasantly at her, keeping the cabin cruiser wide open. 'If I had a bugle, I'd be the cavalry!'

She pushed herself further into the towelling wrap and further into the corner. It was perfectly plain that she had come to the conclusion that Bodie was a right nutter.

Bodie's walkie-talkie spluttered and Doyle's voice crackled out.

'There's a low roof opposite a large white wall ...'

Bodie looked ahead along the cut, seeing the walls and the leaning trees, the glint of water, the skyline jagged with rooftops. A large white wall ...

'Once we reach that roof,' came Doyle's voice. 'We can't hold them.'

Bodie felt the shudder of the boat through his feet. He willed the craft to go faster. A large white wall ... Come on, come on! This was worse than urging traffic lights to change on order ...

He glanced at the woman. There'd be a job for her to do, pretty damn quick. Bodie set about calming her fears and cajoling her into thinking him not quite the nutter he appeared.

The upper room had been barricaded with all the furniture they could haul across the door. Doyle winced as shots slammed into the wood. Going across to the window he looked out, along the canal. More shots slammed from the barricaded door. The gunmen out there were using silenced weapons; but Doyle's and Tinker Bell's shots slashed with ear-splitting concussions. Doyle hefted his walkie-talkie.

'Can you see a girl waving?'

Leia was out on the flat roof, opposite the large white wall. She waved vigorously.

Bodie's voice crackled through. 'I can see her!'

Leia ran back across the roof to the window. 'He's coming!'

'Okay,' shouted Doyle. 'Out!'

44

He bundled Mr X out of the window. The man was shaking with terror. The bodyguard tumbled through last and stationed himself flat against the wall by the window. The other three ran on and took cover behind a narrow ledge. They all heard the smash of the door as it went down scattering the barricading furniture. One of the gunmen stuck his head out of the window, his automatic pointed.

Tinker Bell shot him through the head.

Leia turned away in revulsion. Doyle sent a couple of shots into the window over the sprawled and bloody corpse. He had to keep them penned in there until Bodie reached him.

The staccato splutter of the outboard echoed off the walls. Bodie swirled the boat up towards them. He yelled in a firm controlled voice to the woman in the towelling robe. She held the end of a rope in her elegant fingers.

'Now,' bellowed Bodie. 'Throw it!'

Doyle caught the flung rope and hauled in as Bodie throttled back. Mr X and Leia were assisted on to the deck of the cabin cruiser and crabbed around to drop into the cockpit. Bodie eyed Doyle. Doyle turned back to the flat roof and called out to the bodyguard, spreadeagled against the wall by the window.

'He's on the boat – Now!'

Doyle started shooting at the window. Tinker Bell hesitated. Then he started running for the edge of the roof. His cannon-ball head hunched down. A shot and then a fusillade broke from the window. The bodyguard went on running; but he lurched sideways. His arms flew up. He fell on to his side, and still his legs made running movements as the bullets stitched into him. Bodie appeared over the edge of the roof, smashed a whole clip at the window, yelling.

'You're covered!'

Doyle leaped back and dropped down beside Bodie as slugs cut the air about them. There was no time to spare for Tinker Bell. He was probably dead. Well, he got paid to do his job, and he took the risks, just like they did . . .

45

'Go!' yelled Bodie as they hit the boat.

The woman shoved the throttle all the way open. Bodie had given her a very brief indoctrination talk, and it was paying dividends. Now he shouldered across and took the wheel, telling her to join the others in the cabin.

The cabin cruiser swirled out along the canal. The gunmen on the roof snapped a few parting shots. Then they ran back to the house. The CI5 agents knew they hadn't seen the last of that little lot, not by a long way.

In the cabin Leia, close to Mr X, noticed his hands. Her eyes widened and she quickly pulled off the concealing *hatta*. She gasped. With a tigerish movement she crossed to the doorway and shouted, almost incoherently, to Bodie and Doyle. The face revealed when the concealing *hatta* fell aside was pale and small, sweat-sheened, terrified and yet screwed up by some inner compulsion.

Leia called out angrily. 'This is not Hanish!'

'Who the hell's Hanish?' said Bodie.

'This is some kind of trick!' It was clear Leia just couldn't assimilate whatever it was she had discovered.

'What's she talking about?' said Bodie.

'I don't know,' said his partner.

'Who the hell is she?'

With an odd little lift of his rounded chin, Doyle said: 'You're talking about the woman I love.' He glanced at her, passionate, blazing, wrought up in the doorway. 'Leia.'

The cultured accents of the boat's owner broke in, the fury bubbling out like fizzing champagne. *'Who the hell are all of you?'*

That was a good question – but there was no time to answer it. Bodie snapped a look ahead at the grimy brick bridge spanning the canal. The shiny roofs of cars showed over the parapet and the heads of men looking down.

'Here they are ahead!' yelled Bodie. 'All right. Everybody inside!'

The gunmen climbed on to the parapet. Looking down they saw what appeared to be a deserted cabin cruiser nosing at full throttle towards the centre of the bridge. The boat veered only a little from the middle of the channel. Two gunmen leaped down as the boat passed under, staggered, caught their balances, and as the leader shot down from the bridge to cover them, started for the cabin.

Shots cracked about the deck. Doyle threw himself out of the doorway, rolled on to his back and from that position plugged the first gunman as he tried to claw with one hand to the safety rail and shoot with the other. Bodie smashed glass with the snout of his Browning and shot the second man as he exchanged shots. And, all the time, the fire from the bridge spattered down.

Both gunmen, hit, staggered. They yelped but the engine noise attenuated their yells. They toppled off and in swashes of foam disappeared aft. Leia let out a startled cry. The gunsmoke cleared. Doyle checked the cabin cruiser's deck for any more lice, found it clean, and went back to the cabin.

Leia held her arm and the blood oozed greasily between her fingers. She ignored that, tempestuously shouting at Mr X. She was clearly demanding to know who he was.

Doyle said roughly: 'Are you all right?'

'It's nothing.' Leia took a breath and twin spots of red flamed on her cheeks. 'But *he!* We have been fooled. He is an *impostor!*' Leia looked wild. 'The whole thing is a trick. Maybe it is you two they are trying to kill.' As Bodie and Doyle exchanged wary glances, acknowledging what she said could make sense, she added: 'Don't you know what your assignment is? Or are you just a couple of dumb bodyguards?'

The two CI5 men felt the pressures, felt the dangers, and, also, they felt something else. Outside Bodie said to Doyle: 'She's nagging us.'

Defensively, Doyle said. 'She's stopped a bullet.'

Leia called out vehemently: 'You are being used. Both of you!'

'Maybe she's right?' Bodie's eyebrows drew down.

'Look – ' Doyle's angry whisper just carried. 'We got our

assignment. All the way along someone's been tipping someone off.'

'Who could that be?'

'Why did Cowley shake our hands?'

Bodie's thoughts churned like a sewer filled with filth. 'We're expendable . . . Cowley? But why?'

'We'll finish our assignment.' Doyle's lips drew back and his round cheerful face took on that devilish look. His hair was a mess, as usual when he was in action. 'We'll deliver our man. Then – we'll find out.'

The compact was made. 'Right,' said Bodie.

The Middle Eastern gunmen acted now with a reckless lack of caution. They sensed their quarry was close to the kill. Working like maniacs they detached a narrow boat from her companions along the bank and swung her diagonally across the canal. The channel was effectively blocked. The cabin cruiser motoring around the bend by the glassy-sheening brick wall of a warehouse almost piled headlong into the narrow boat.

Instant action avoided the collision and Bodie hurled the boat backwards in a churning wash of foam. The cruiser vanished around the bend. The gunmen, shouting to one another, ran back to reach the bank and chase up towards the warehouse.

Bodie and Doyle had to abandon the boat. She had served well; but now they had to abandon ship. They used the anchor to fix a line to the warehouse roof and, the CI5 men working overtime, the party was deposited on the roof. Bodie looked down on the voluptuous form of the woman in her towelling robe.

'Look,' he said. 'I can explain everything –'

The woman looked not so much exasperated as helpless. 'What about the damage to my boat?'

'You'll be compensated.'

'Who is going to compensate me?'

'What's your phone number?'

'485 6325.'

Doyle let out a shout around then and Bodie, looking quickly across the roof, spotted the dark agile forms of the gunmen. He shouted down to the woman: 'What's your name?'

'Quick,' yelped Doyle, and started shepherding Mr X and Leia away.

'I'll tell you,' said the woman. 'When you call.'

Bodie started along the parapet after the others, and then halted. He yelled down: 'Who will I ask for?'

'Philippa.'

Bodie waved down and ran off. To himself, in disbelief, he said: 'Philippa!'

Over on the far side of the warehouse roof they organised a way down. A drainpipe was used, and Bodie slung Mr X around his neck, gripping on like a monkey, whilst Doyle took Leia down. A driverless van with open doors stood, waiting, it seemed, for them to arrive. The driver was off delivering groceries by the look of it. They piled in and Bodie started up. This section of the operation went far too smoothly to last.

Ominous figures appeared around the corner of the warehouse as the van drove towards the cross-street. The van driver catapulted out of the doorway to their rear, yelling and waving his arms. Bodie drove sharply, not too fast, and the gunmen abruptly faded. The leader flipped out a radio handset and gabbled swiftly into it. The van drove on as the gunmen ran back towards the canal.

For the moment the CI5 men with Mr X and Leia were running free; but they were all aware that the opposition had not given up. That mystifying and infuriating source of information wouldn't give in now, either.

Doyle flipped his walkie-talkie on. 'Escort One and Two calling Big Daddy, over.'

Cowley's voice answered. Doyle went on: 'We are returning the hot potato. We can't say where we are because maybe we don't exist.'

The splutter on the R/T made Doyle's spirits rise. 'Now listen to me –' started off George Cowley.

'We have a hot potato on our hands – it's been burning our fingers. We're going to put it back where we found it. If the bucket isn't there in twenty minutes we're going to throw it in the water.'

Bodie leaned forward and Doyle slanted the R/T for him.

'And,' said Bodie. 'The bucket better have its engines going when we get there.'

Doyle said: 'Over and out.'

That, the partners both felt, should have sorted out a few priorities. As for George Cowley, his hard manner covered a multitude of sins, and one of them was neatly expressed as he said, under his breath and entirely to himself: 'Good lads!'

They saw no sign of the opposition on the way to the docks and, given the way the CI5 men had figured this shambles, that did not surprise them. As the van turned into the last long and narrow road leading down into the dock area Bodie looked ahead through the windscreen. In his resigned, sarcastic way, he said: 'Surprise, surprise.'

Halfway along and just past the yawning shadow of a warehouse a car had been positioned diagonally across the road completely blocking the way ahead. Another car angled off reinforcing the road block. The gunmen were there, too, and the shadows cut down across the scene, hard-edged with menace.

Bodie saw the open warehouse to the side, the hanging doors drawn up, he allowed for the geography of the place, and he swung the wheel violently. 'Okay! Here goes!'

The tyres on the van screeched like banshees as Bodie slewed into the open warehouse. The shadows clamped down. They howled along through a vast emptiness, seeing the crossbeams flickering away like railway sleepers. The van jounced over obstructions. The people in the back were flung about like kiddies on a helter-skelter. A wall of packing cases reared at the far end. Bodie trampled all over the accelerator and the van smashed into the wooden crates, burst through, went flaring out on to the quay beyond like a motor-bike shooting the flaming circle, shedding crates which clattered away across the damp stones.

The van hissed into a semi-circle, the tyres screaming, and then Bodie stamped on the brakes. The van skidded the last few yards and came to a shuddering halt with its nose pointing away and at the gunmen who were running down the road past the warehouse, and its rear yawning out over the steps leading down to the landing stage and the launch. The launch was there, engines running as Bodie had said, the sailors waiting.

Mr X was carried forcibly off the back of the van as Bodie hollered: 'Loose those moorings!'

Now the gunmen were kneeling to shoot. Bullets cracked and splattered against the front of the van. Doyle returned the fire as Bodie bundled Mr X down the steps to the launch.

The launch rocked. Her engines opened up with a full-throated roar. She surged away, spilling white water from her flanks, tearing out across the dock. Bodie sprinted back up the steps and loosed a couple of shots at the gunmen. The leader, the one with the fierce fanatical face, couldn't seem to understand just what had happened to his carefully laid plans. He took a few running steps across the quay, as though pursuing the launch, shooting hopelessly. Then he stopped. He stood quite still.

Doyle climbed down from the van and stood by Bodie. Both agents put away their guns.

The leader of the Middle Eastern gunmen lowered his own weapon, and spoke a few words. His men climbed to their feet, put away their guns. A most weird sensation afflicted Bodie and Doyle, and they were aware they shared the feeling and were confident that the same sensation was felt by the opposition.

Only one word described that odd little moment – hiatus.

Then the leader made an eloquent foreign shrug, a slumping lift and fall of the shoulders. He turned and with his men slouched off. Most odd . . .

Doyle said: 'You *have* to say it for him . . .'

Bodie said: 'He *did* try . . .'

The words – not so much patronising as admitting a tough adversary's skill and final defeat – were not glib. But that was over and done with. Now, there were other words to be said and Doyle and Bodie intended to have them said, come what may.

They saw that Leia was properly treated in the CI5 hospital and the wound in her arm would heal cleanly and quickly. Then in the corridor outside her room they confronted George Cowley . . .

'Yes,' Cowley told them, quite unrepentant. 'He was a fake. We knew he was a fake. We set up the whole operation. Now, thanks to you two, we have been able to identify virtually the entire secret army of a certain – nation – built up within these shores. When the real Dr Hanish does visit this country – and that is a diplomatic matter which is none of our business – we will be able to guarantee his safety.'

Very quietly, Doyle said: 'May I point out one thing, sir? The whole scheme could have had another purpose – to make a certain nation think that Hanish visited us, when he didn't . . .'

The pause Cowley let into the conversation could have been fraught with all kinds of blasts and thunderbolts. But he simply said: 'Very shrewd of you.' His mouth pinched in on the word shrewd; it was a word that fitted George Cowley. 'A speculation above and beyond the call of duty.' His smile would have glaciated a volcano. Doyle went on talking stoutly.

'Which being the case – anyone who learned of this charade would be a possible security weakness?'

'But who has – apart from yourselves?'

'The lady,' said Doyle. 'Leia.'

'Ahh,' said Cowley, and the smile warmed perceptibly. With an officiousness that sat without incongruity on his ex-policeman's image, Doyle said: 'With your authority, sir, I shall stay to interrogate her.'

Cowley kept his smile and turned away to leave. 'Remember, there's only one way to interrogate a lady – over dinner.'

As Cowley left, highly satisfied, Doyle winked at Bodie.

'Wait a minute,' said Bodie. He sounded aggrieved and his handsome face screwed up into comic thought-lines. 'I saved her life – with yours.'

With an infuriating smirk, Doyle said: 'Then you can't interrogate. You're emotionally involved!'

With that Doyle strode jauntily back into the room where Leia and her bandaged arm waited for him. Bodie looked down the corridor at the retreating form of Cowley. He was left isolated, in the middle.

He shook his head at the villainy of the world.

Suddenly he looked up. His smooth forehead corrugated in intense thought. His famous eyebrows drew down as he struggled to recall a vital piece of information. To himself he said: '485 – 23 – 65?'

Chapter Four

Although not always dressed with tailored smartness, Bodie was always dressed in impeccable taste. His quiet good grooming gave him an essentially English air of elegance. Because tonight was a special night, and Claire was a special lady, Bodie's suit was a marvel of exquisite cut and he fitted the candle-lit intimate surroundings of the expensive restaurant perfectly.

Claire's natural blonde hair caught gleams from the candles, and laughter danced entrancingly in her eyes as she responded to Bodie. He leaned forward over the table. All about them the sounds of talk and laughter, the clink of cutlery, the chiming of glass and bottle, enclosed the two, as it were in a dome of intimate privacy. Her white blouse was cut as perfectly as Bodie's suit, her face was as alive as his, her happiness at the prospects of the evening ahead matched his own.

With a smile and a half-dismissive gesture Bodie rose, throwing his napkin on to the tablecloth, excusing himself for the telephone call he was duty bound to make.

Claire watched him walking with that easy lithe grace between the crowded tables, passing with a football-player's unconscious swerve the waiter who plodded on carrying an immense cellophane-wrapped and be-ribboned sheaf of flowers. Claire smiled again as Bodie went out of the door towards the phone booths.

The noise of the restaurant faded as Bodie picked up the phone. His finger poised to dial CI5 H.Q. He was making a real and genuine effort to think about CI5 and crime-busting and George Cowley's impossible demands, and, for a tiny moment, to push aside his eager and alive thoughts of Claire.

The side of the telephone booth leaped at him.

The roof disappeared.

Dust and dirt billowed about him like a sandstorm, choking him, flinging grit into his eyes.

The explosion smashed in a giant wave of concussion, impossible noise engulfing him and the tearing blast hurling him full length. The world seemed to have blown up.

He was on the floor, the phone still in his hand and the wrenched-off wire trailing.

The screams began soon afterwards.

He started to get up, and fell forward, and pushed himself up with his arms straight, feeling the phone biting into his hand. Commotion and screaming and continuing smashing destruction as blasted walls fell and glasses crashed down dazed him. His head rang like all the bells in the head of Quasimodo. He staggered towards the door of the restaurant as the smoke billowed out. He struggled in. Shattered glass lay like a second carpet. His shoes crunched. Smoke half-blinded him. The yelling and the screams roiled around him as the tortured souls of Hell must shriek in agony.

A white-painted trellis had been torn down and twisted askew. The table had been blown God-knew-where. He stumbled forward and looked down.

'Claire! Claire!'

She was still there. She lay sprawled in the obscene wreckage, her clothes blackened and ripped, her face wet with blood. She did not move. Her body looked shrivelled, twisted, shrunken.

Bodie dropped to his knees. He did not touch her. He

looked down and his face was the face of a man in torment.

He didn't even notice the dust and soot fouling that beautiful suit, the rips in the elegant trousers as he knelt by her side. His feelings were there, inside him, like the waters of a lake about to burst the dam that pent them in.

'Claire,' he said, and shut his eyes.

George Cowley was sometimes referred to as a man who did not know what humanity was. That was a gross libel. But, here and now, standing in the middle of what had been a restaurant, he had to banish all trite feelings of outrage and grief. His brief was simple, handed to him by the government through the committee set up by the Home Secretary when he had formed CI5, simple; but devilishly difficult to implement. Bombings – his job, if bombings could not be prevented, was to apprehend the bombers so that they, at least, would not murder more innocent people. And, this was just one part of his case load.

He glanced through photographs clenched in one hand. 'No warning – nothing!'

Ray Doyle said: 'I.R.A.? Another wave of bombings?'

Cowley limped across the rubble, looking at the photographs. 'I want a check-list on everybody here yesterday.'

'Everybody?' Doyle moved through the mess with his chief.

'Staff, tradesmen, deliveries, all table reservations – '

Doyle handed across the list he had already prepared. Cowley favoured him with a look that told Doyle that the chief was only a little surprised and quietly pleased at the efficiency. Doyle suppressed his smile. 'Everybody who set foot in here except the passing trade.'

Among the uniformed policemen and firemen working in the wreckage a movement by what had been the window took Cowley's attention. Instantly, George Cowley limped forward.

'Bodie! I'm not having you on this case.'

Bodie had washed and changed – after he'd seen Claire to hospital. She'd seemed tiny in the white bed, heavily bandaged, unconscious, but not, thank God, dead. Now he spoke heavily to the chief of CI5.

'Just passing. Thought I'd call by and –'

'I mean what I say. You're emotionally involved.'

'Two people dead, eleven seriously injured.' Bodie's nostrils whitened and he began to lose his cool. 'How many is it supposed to be before you're allowed to become emotionally involved?'

Cowley took a breath. His face screwed down. 'I'm not arguing. I'm sorry. You know that. Deeply sorry.'

Bodie nodded. He was again indrawn, thoughtful, as though his mind was working independently of his actions. Without another word he turned away and walked off. Cowley looked after him, a frown dinting his forehead, and Doyle said: 'If you want my personal opinion, sir –'

'I don't.'

'I was only going to suggest –'

' – the bomb might have been intended for Bodie.' Cowley nodded decisively. 'Quite. Which is another reason for not wanting him on the case.'

The hotel was neat and inconspicuous, just on the edge of the West End; the clientele were neat and inconspicuous, and Macneil, an American, being by nature neat and inconspicuous, blended perfectly. Which suited him. In his hotel suite he threw down the daily paper with a disgusted snort. The bomb had gone off, the restaurant had been wrecked; but the names of the casualties did not include the name he wished to find there.

'What do we have to do to get this guy?' he complained to Phipps, who stood patiently by the armchair. 'Mount an air raid?'

Dressed like a business executive, with dark glossy hair and a face that concealed his thoughts, Phipps maintained his patience. 'A bullet would have been easier.'

'Better,' Macneil told him, 'if it looks political. Better if the target is obscured.'

'Messy, though.'

'Squeamish, Mr Phipps?' Macneil lifted his orange juice.

'If I were, I wouldn't be in this racket.'

Macneil glanced up, half-frowning, the orange juice poised.

'Quaint, old-fashioned term. This is a business, Mr Phipps.'

Going into the hospital Bodie determined that he would not be depressed by the institutional smell, the air of efficiency and scrubbed cleanliness, the anonymous trolleys parked here and there, the nurses, themselves scrubbed and clean, the multicoloured signs, the general atmosphere of impersonal personal service. He checked on Claire and was told there was no change, and then, probably breaking a quantity of rules, made his way to the ward where Gino, the restaurant owner, lay shielded by screens.

Gino's face was still white. But the plaster across his forehead gleamed whiter still. His bruises and scratches would disappear and his head would heal; but a deep wound had been inflicted on his spirit.

'I don't know why anyone should do this. I tell them I don't care about politics. I run a restaurant.'

'I know – but someone –'

'Signore Bodie – why me? Why my restaurant?'

'Okay, okay. Now, just before the explosion some flowers were delivered –'

'That's right.' Gino's face reflected the passion he felt for his restaurant, the years he had spent building his reputation. 'By special delivery – for your table.'

'Was I mentioned by name?'

'Table ten. That's all. I think, because you are with the young lady –'

'All right, all right. Now, you gave me that particular table because you'd had a last-minute cancellation. Right?'

'That's right. I was very busy, you saw how busy I was –'

Bodie saw Gino was close to tears at the disaster, at the memories; quick, hot Latin tears . . .

Bodie spoke firmly, trying to prevent the scene from

becoming too unbearable. 'Do you remember the name of the cancellation?'

'I remember.' Gino swallowed. 'It was for his wedding anniversary. But then he doesn't come, so I give the table to you.'

'Gino – try and remember his name. It's important.'

'He came many time – Mr Forrest, I think that was it.'

Bodie drew a breath and leaned back, looking up, and saw Ray Doyle standing by the door staring hard at him. His face tightened. He bent swiftly to Gino. 'Listen, Gino. Let's keep it just between us. What I was asking you? You know?'

Doyle, now that he had been seen, moved in as Bodie, lifting his voice, said: 'Take care, Gino. Ciao.'

The partners moved away from the white-sheeted bed and confronted each other by the glass partition doors. Doyle looked hot about the cheeks.

'What the hell d'you think you're – '

'He's a mate,' said Bodie, curtly. 'I can see a mate in hospital when I want, can't I, without you or Cowley breathing down my – '

'Don't!' Doyle broke in. 'I know what you're doing here.'

'Just don't hassle me, Doyle.'

'You great clown!' They walked side by side along the disinfected corridor. 'Don't you think I know what you're going through? Just don't blow it for yourself by – '

'I,' said Bodie with an ugly note in his voice, 'am not going to drop it!'

'I'm not asking you to. I know you too well. And if Cowley finds out – '

Bodie turned on him. 'You want to do me a favour? You want to help? Then just stay clear of me. I'm going to get whoever did it – and there's nothing you or Cowley, anybody, can do to stop me!'

Ray Doyle understood all that, it was obvious. He admitted to a sly surmise about just how much notice Cowley thought Bodie would take of the warnings. The two men hurried out of the hospital, with Bodie striding on and Doyle trying to get his point over as they hustled past the busy traffic of the casualty entrance. 'Will you just stop for a minute?' yelped Doyle. 'Just stop and talk for a minute?'

Bodie ignored his partner. Doyle danced around in front in exasperation and then grabbed Bodie's shoulder and hauled him up. 'Bodie! Do I have to fight before I even talk to you? You want to get yourself arrested for brawling in public? Fine – go right ahead. There's nothing Cowley'd like better than to see you safely locked up 'til this is all over.'

They glared at each other, eyeball to eyeball, the fair-haired one and the dark-haired one, the scruffy and the elegant. Then Bodie let out a sigh, and Doyle – who had never thought the likelihood a possibility – knew their partnership had not been irretrievably broken.

'Don't worry,' said Bodie. And with a flash of his old arrogant cynicism: 'I won't embarrass anyone.'

Doyle watched him climb into his silver-grey Capri, the dents and scratches all beautifully polished out, and he shook his head, a tiny smile of amusement and resignation curving up those lips that had been clamped in hot determination. They were a team, Bodie and Doyle, and not even CI5 could foul that up – not now . . .

Although much-publicised remarks by highly thought of police commissioners might lead Joe Q. Public to the belief that the police were overwhelmed by a tide of crime, forensic science continued to slog along feeling collars. One of the waiters from the restaurant – he had been in the kitchen at the time and had taken a pan of spaghetti in the face but was otherwise unharmed – recognised one of the several hundred mugshots shown to him in the interview room of the local nick. The news was flashed through to CI5 and Cowley briefed Doyle.

'Name of Arthur Brian Pendle – picked up for drug dealing and illegal possession of firearms. Sent down for three years.'

The photograph showed a rat-faced man in his mid-twenties, sleek and polished, yes; but narrow, mean, hypertense.

'One of the dailies had a call allegedly from the I.R.A. claiming responsibility,' said Cowley, flicking the picture with a manicured fingernail. 'Whoever it was hadn't done their homework properly.'

'No code – ?'

'Precisely. Someone's trying to make it look like a political bombing – and it wasn't. Sending a bouquet of flowers? Much too theatrical.'

Doyle didn't mention Bodie. He rather wanted the old man to keep his thoughts away from that explosive subject. 'Pendle,' said Doyle. 'Arthur Brian Pendle.'

Bodie wasted no time. He tooled the Capri out to Forrest's house and nodded to himself as the wealth of the neighbourhood came into sight. It took money to live here. The Forrest house was red brick, long and low, a single-storey house almost a ranch type, but lacking the vulgarities of that species of residence. With adequate internal plumbing it was a house that would be regarded as typically English by a typical American. Bodie sat in his car for a quarter of an hour watching, then he got out and walked up the drive and rang the bell. The daughter of the house answered, brown-eyed, brown-haired, a tennis-type girl, and she directed him to her mother in the garden. Bodie sauntered around, casually, forcing himself to relax.

Mrs Madge Forrest looked to be around forty or so, still remarkably attractive, with an open fearless face. She wore a pink blouse and an orange casual cardigan, and jeans. Her gardening gloves were bright yellow, and she looked as though she knew how to use the secateurs she carried.

She sighed as Bodie explained.

'I suppose it had to happen. When we saw the paper we were shocked. Brian said you'd ask. It is about the bombing? Am I right?'

'I made a list at St Catherine's House; couples with the

name Forrest who'd have had wedding anniversaries on – that – day. Quite a short list. Just you.'

Madge Forrest was impressed by this explanation. Bodie had been in and out of St Catherine's House like a fireman, yanking the big tome down and racing through the entries. Then he'd driven straight here. 'Well, I don't know how I'm going to be able to help you, Mr – ?'

'Bodie. I suppose the first thing is why didn't you and your husband show up after you'd booked the table?'

'By the time Brian got in, it was late, so rather than go through all the effort of driving up to London, we decided to have a small celebration at home. Brian is a chartered accountant with an office in London – and, well, the travel sometimes –'

'I don't suppose you can think of a reason why someone should want to kill him?'

Madge Forrest stared at Bodie as though he had sprouted horns. She barely believed she'd heard him aright. 'Brian? Kill him? Oh, no . . . Not Brian.'

'Why's that?'

She flustered up at this. 'Well . . . no, it's absolutely too ridiculous for words.'

'Mrs Forrest. Someone sent that bomb to your table specifically, table number ten. Now, why do you think that was?'

The flustered woman abruptly became positive. 'It's absolutely nothing to do with Brian – or me, if that's what you're thinking, Mr Bodie. We weren't even there!'

The heavy seductive scent of the roses reached Bodie as he made his goodbyes. He was not altogether happy about Madge Forrest's answers; but for the moment he had to look elsewhere. This house, this garden, the wealth here – that could do with a little checking out. He took himself off to his Capri and a fast run back to town.

In the heart of the smoke Ray Doyle was following up the elusive and erratic trail of Arthur Pendle. The man had a sister and Doyle turned up her address from a girl at the place she had last worked. Authority had categorised Pendle as a vicious little swine, without the knowledge necessary to construct the kind of bomb the squad had deduced had wrecked the restaurant. He'd wangled parole, and the parole officer was swamped with paper work and a caseload no man should have to carry single-handed. Doyle went off to the address of Pendle's sister in the frame of mind of a man turning over a haystack without a magnet.

Bodie's Capri hummed back along concrete roads that led through that part of the world that was neither town nor country, a place of withdrawn houses, isolated telephone boxes, the occasional bus, many trees and the intimate twee pub. The road led on to the outer suburbs of London. Before long Bodie's nose twitched. His mirror told him that the black Triumph was following him like the tail stuck to a kite.

Bodie's mobile lips drew back.

A little experiment seemed in order . . .

He swung the car left-handed into a crossroad and bowled along. In due time the Triumph appeared in his mirror. Bodie let his Capri roll on at the same steady speed until the next road turning appeared. The cars rose and fell as the road wound over folds in the ground. Tyres hissed gently. The trees lining the road passed backwards sedately.

Then, Bodie hit the accelerator.

The Capri howled ahead, picking up speed fast, belted along the road and swirled savagely around the corner and into Partingale Lane. Dust and leaves cyconed up as the tyres screeched. The Triumph shot into view in the mirror, chasing him in earnest now. The cars screamed along the road.

Bodie hit the next corner late and fast, trampling on the brakes, skidding the Capri into a sliding smother. He was barely conscious of the surroundings, seeing only the corner of the road to his rear. The Capri halted, shuddering. Bodie was out of the car, the Browning auto in both

63

fists poised and aimed over the roof, his feet spread and his body braced in the pose. He lined up the gun on that corner – and waited.

And waited ...

The gun held straight at the corner. Nothing happened. He waited ...

Presently he sucked in a breath of air and relaxed a trifle. And became aware of the bus stop on the other side of the road, and the queue of about a dozen people: housewives, elderly retired folk, a parson, all waiting for their bus and staring at him in open-mouthed amazement.

He straightened up a little. He became aware of the gun in his fists. There was no sign that the black Triumph had ever existed. He felt suddenly remarkably exposed. Here he was, brandishing a gun, taking cover behind his car, in the middle of a quiet suburban road – and, to complete his embarrassment the bus queue entered into the spirit of the scene.

One by one they started to clap him.

He saw them gazing at him, saw their faces, and he saw and heard their hands, giving him a well-merited round of applause.

Bodie stepped back from his car, the gun still held up in his fists, and the bus queue clapped and clapped.

The council block of flats made the usual impression on Doyle as he moved along the corridor towards Sally Pendle's door. He and Bodie had visited far too many squalid places like this for them to continue to react with horror; if people chose to live like this, or were forced to live like this, that was their concern and their problem. The concrete walls were covered in graffiti, litter was strewn everywhere, the red and apple green paint peeling from the rows of identical doors. The dustbins looked as though Arsenal had kicked them around a bit in preparation for Manchester United. A rusty bike might have been rideable; it was lethal to whoever tried. Kids yelled and screeched and the smell of cabbages and other unidentifiable aromas floated through the close air. Doyle found the door and rang the bell. He expected a wait and he was not disappointed. Presently, the door opened six inches.

'Sally Pendle?'

She eyed him with the flat dweller's habitual suspicion of unexpected knocks or rings on doors. She was a blonde, of sorts, with blue eyes that should not, probably, have looked on all the things they had witnessed. She wore a dark blue dress. Doyle summed it all up, her manner, the way her hand held the door. He went on with his smile in evidence, smoothly: 'I'm a friend of Arthur's. Ray Doyle's the name. We were inside together.'

She said, quickly, on a breath – far too quickly and on a breath that caught in her throat – 'I don't know where he is.'

Easily, Doyle said: 'I thought you might know – being his sister.'

'I told you. I don't know where he is. What do you want with him, anyway?'

'I owe him some money.' Well, it had worked before, it might always work again.

A door closed inside the flat. Doyle eased himself around, facing the girl. 'All right,' she said, and her eyes moved sideways, showing the whites. 'You give it to me. I'll see he gets it.'

Doyle's smile widened. 'Ah . . . I'd rather give it to him personally, if you don't mind.'

'I've told you.' The sharpness of tone was unmistakable. 'I'll see he gets it.'

'Right,' said Doyle. 'You do that!' and without warning he thrust the door wide open and dashed past Sally Pendle. He charged into the flat, seeing the tawdry ordinariness of its chain-store furnishings, hearing Sally's piercing scream from the door. That scream was no simple reaction to his sudden move; that was a warning signal. Doyle bashed through into the kitchen – empty – the passage – empty – the bathroom – empty. Sally was there, clinging to him, shrieking hysterically, kicking him, trying to scratch him,

5   65

a wild cat in a dark blue dress with blonde hair all over the place.

'Who are you?' she shrieked as she hacked at his shins and tried to gouge out his eye. 'Get out of here! You've no right to break in here. I'll call the police.' He had to take a wrist away from his face, for the fingernail was decidedly dangerous. 'You get the hell out of here!' she screamed. 'I'm warning you!'

A door slammed. Footsteps running. Doyle attempted to make for the passage again and Sally hung on to him like a despairing tackler hanging on to a flying threequarter.

'*Arthur!*'

Doyle had to put her aside most firmly. She clung like a burr. He heard the front door go and then managed at last to free himself from the screaming kicking girl. Out of the door and along the concrete corridor, a real concrete jungle, down the cracked stairs, past all the mess and rubbish – hurdling a dustbin – he spotted Arthur Pendle flying across the low wall of the kiddies' playground.

He wore a dark brown anorak and jeans, and he was fairly leaping along and if he did not knock a child bowling over like a ninepin then it was by mere luck and not through any concern for the kiddies.

Doyle hared after him.

For only a single instant Sally Pendle stared after her brother who fled in such panic from this hateful overbearing man with the mop of curls and the fierce and ferocious manner cloaked under an infectious smile. Then she dashed back into the flat and snatched at the phone, dialling out in blind panic to a well-known number . . .

Over the far wall Arthur Pendle clambered like a commando and headed across the wasteland fringing the railway tracks. Following across the scrubby ground with clumps of dispirited grass and areas of garbage strewn about, Doyle abruptly realised he could be in the middle of a wild and open moorland – incredible, with the tower blocks on the horizon and the railway yards curving away on the other side. But here among the dry grasses and scrub and the heaps of junk was another world.

Pendle fled madly between heaped banks of scrub-covered ground, hurdling remains of cars and perambulators, dodging between tottering piles of rubble and detritus. His breath laboured in his lungs. Doyle ran easily and smoothly, catching the tearaway, ready to feel his collar.

With the suddenness of a broken film Pendle ran between ferny banks towards a monstrous pile of rubble and wreckage and, abruptly, shockingly, saw there was no way through. He was trapped.

Doyle sprinted up and was incongruously aware of the splashes of red and blue of flowers nestling among the greenery. Pendle stared about, his narrow face twitching, saw an iron angle bar in the rubble, snatched it out. He hefted it like a club. His face sheened sweat and his lips ricked back.

'Stay away from me or I'll kill you!'

Doyle checked his pace but continued to close in. Pendle crabbed away to the side and attempted to angle around Doyle and so reach the gravelly track leading between the ferny banks to the tip. Doyle moved lithely to intercept him and heard the sound of a car engine from the rear. The iron bar lifted. Doyle risked a quick glance back and saw a dark saloon car heading up the gravel, lurching and bumping. He switched his gaze back in time to catch sight of Arthur Pendle hurling forward enraged, the iron bar lifted, every intention of smashing Doyle's brains out written madly on his contorted face.

The car had to be ignored for the moment – there was no sign it was the police.

The angle iron looked edged and hard, a wicked weapon.

Pendle let rip a tremendous shriek of passion as he struck.

Doyle ducked and went in low, not caring if he went in low and dirty, just wanting to get this maniac under control before the idiot splashed Doyle's brains all over the pretty flowers and the ferns and the junk littering the ground.

He hit Pendle in the guts, grasping him, rushing him back. The iron bar flew up into the air. It somersaulted and landed with a clang across a broken crate of non-returnable bottles which smashed into a million diamonds among the dirt.

With insane strength Pendle kicked himself free from Doyle and lurched gaspingly for the iron bar.

Doyle gritted down the pain stabbing at him from Pendle's kick and went after him.

He flung himself forward and Pendle staggered away, yelling. There was the roaring sound of a car's engine.

The sound of rubber tyres on the gravel crunched like bones being splintered.

The smell of tar rose about Doyle as he skidded on wetness and staggered, still trying to close with Pendle who backed off, shaking and yelling.

Ray Doyle was aware with a small part of his mind of the flowers and the scrub and the dirt and the junk being above him, and the sky beneath him. A great and soggy pain enveloped his back and side. He was in the air. The pain thumped him cruelly.

The dark saloon car, swerving quite deliberately across the gravel track, hit him full on. Doyle flew up into the air like a tossed sheaf of grain, somersaulted, crashed on and over to skid along his cheek and side into a patch of bushes, sending dirt cascading away.

He lay there, crumpled on his side, his face pressed into the dirt.

He did not move.

Chapter Five

Arthur Pendle staggered up and stood, shaking, his sweating face still locked into that hate-filled rictus of willing murder.

The car shuddered to a stop. Peter Crabbe got out quickly, a dark-haired man in his early forties with the squat tough build of a fighter, and with the face of a professional gambler, smooth and secretive. He looked angrily across at Pendle and then hurried over to the crumpled body of the man he had just knocked flying. His driving had been rather good. Pendle drew a deep breath and joined him and, together, they stood looking down.

'A cop?' demanded Crabbe.

'Think so.'

'Think so! What d'you mean, think so? Why'd you run for it if you didn't know?'

Pendle swallowed and tried to stop his gasping shuddering.

'He is! He's got to be.'

'Let's get him in the car —'

'No!' screamed Pendle. 'Let's leave him!'

Crabbe looked disgusted. 'Get him in the car.'

For a moment the silence locked them together, then Pendle let out his breath, and bent towards the crumpled body. Crabbe grunted. Together, they lifted the unconscious man and carried him across to the car.

Peter Crabbe had long experience in dealing with tearaways; but this Arthur Pendle was a right nutter. Crabbe wore an off-white suit which lent him an air of distinction. His dark hair was cropped short and his chin, despite ritual shavings, remained blue. He was altogether one tough cookie.

He shoved the unconscious man into the back of the saloon and Pendle got into the front seat. Gently, the car eased out of the wasteland, the tyres crunching on gravel as the tyres of a hearse crunch on the way to the cemetery.

Before Bodie continued his obstinate checking of Brian Forrest he put through a call to the hospital. They told him there was no change in Claire's condition. He put the phone down and looked up at the office block where the offices of Forrest and Padgett awaited his further enquiry. Claire . . . No, there was no way they would stop him from going on with this thing, no way at all.

He went into the entrance and was checking out the name plates when the black car eased into sight and halted over the way. The two men inside sat quietly watching the office block.

Bodie went up to the office where Richard Padgett, Forrest's partner, responded to the initial enquiries with something of a pompous resignation. He excused himself for a moment and left the office. Bodie looked at the photographs on the wall and in a group taken at some businessmen's luncheon saw the pictured representation of Padgett sitting next to a man with the indrawn and whimsical expression of a man accustomed to his own thoughts. He had greying hair and was around fifty. That, surmised Bodie, was Forrest. Padgett came back, smiling fatly.

'Brian Forrest is my partner, Mr Bodie. I find it highly unethical talking about him behind his back.'

'When you're talking about planting bombs in crowded restaurants, Mr Padgett, ethics become a little absurd.'

Padgett smoothed his slicked-back silver hair. He was stout and rubicund, a little bouncy; Bodie saw him as the usual run of professional man – and yet?

'Quite, I realise that,' said Padgett. 'All the same, when he told me you were at his house asking his wife about – '

Bodie broke in. 'You met Forrest about twenty years ago?'

With an irritable sigh, Padgett said: 'Someone introduced us, I can't remember who. Someone who knew I was thinking of starting up on my own.'

Bodie continued on: 'Forrest looked like he'd be the perfect partner?'

'He certainly had all the right contacts. All he ever seemed to have to do was pick up the phone.'

Bodie nodded and moved across the office to glance down out of the window. 'What about his background before he met you?' Down there in the street parked on the other side was a black car. Bodie frowned thoughtfully.

Padgett was talking. 'Been living in the States, mainly. Went there just after his parents died.'

'You handle some pretty big accounts, I'd imagine?'

'Certainly nothing to warrant a bombing, Mr Bodie.'

The green phone on the desk rang and Padgett answered. 'Yes? Fine. Put it through to the other office.' He looked up at Bodie as he put the phone down. 'Would you excuse me for just a moment?' And he hurried with his portly waddle from his office.

This all seemed perfectly straightforward and above-board. A working partnership of twenty years' standing. But that bomb had been sent quite deliberately to the table Forrest had booked and then had not used. The bomb could have been meant for Bodie himself; but the timing was too perfect for that. Bodie scowled at the closed door beyond which Padgett was taking his phone call.

Padgett sat down at the desk in his partner's office before he picked up the phone. 'George? Thanks for ringing me back. Sorry to disturb you but I've got some chap in my office asking a lot of questions. Claims he's something to do with CI5 – is it? Thought if anyone'd know anything about it, you would. Name of Bodie.'

The white Rover 3500 was being chauffeured through the London traffic and George Cowley was speaking on the radio telephone. His face as he listened to Padgett drew down into lines that boded no good for a certain CI5 operative.

'Bodie . . . ? That's all right, Dick. Thanks for checking with me. Do you think I could have a word with him?'

Padgett put the phone down gently and his fat face expressed pleased anticipation. He crossed to his own office, saying: 'Mr Bodie?'

But Bodie had gone.

The porter on duty at the entrance to the office block had seen them all in his time. When Bodie planted himself in front and dangled a set of car keys, the porter waited to hear what mess he was in, a mess that the porter would have to sort out.

'Excuse me – Forrest and Padgett on the fifth floor. Mr Forrest's just asked me to move his car. It is the black one over there across the road, isn't it?'

This was a new one to the porter. He looked puzzled. 'Black?'

They moved together to the glass doors and Bodie said again: 'Black. Just across the road –'

They looked out. The black car was no longer there.

The porter shook his head and decided he'd better remain polite. You never knew. 'Black – no, no. Mr Forrest drives a green car –' He jerked his thumb. 'When he's in town he leaves it in the underground car park.'

Bodie nodded, saying: 'Thank you,' and walked off towards the car park; but he was puzzling over that confounded black car. A tail on a kite? One minute it was there and the next it was gone – decidedly odd.

He'd check out Forrest's green car. The entrance to the underground car park with its warning light and barrier and the harshly-painted signs among the concrete was guarded by a little sentry box. Bodie spoke to the attendant who looked as bored as a pipeline. 'Excuse me – Mr Forrest's car? He asked me if I'd pick it up for him.'

'Mr Forrest?' The attendant shared the porter's view that he had habitually to deal with half-wits. 'He's just this minute gone in to pick it up himself.'

Bodie felt his jaw stiffen. But he wasn't an ace CI5 operative for nothing and the stab of self-sarcasm warmed him.

'Ah, well,' he said, looking wise. 'He must have forgotten he gave me his keys. Whereabouts is he parked?'

'To the left as you go in – far end.'

Bodie gave the attendant a friendly wave and strolled down the ramp. The lights pocked the concrete roof and walls like manic fireflies. Quite a number were unlit. He vanished down the ramp and a moment or two later the black car eased into view on the other side of the road and halted a few metres short of the entrance.

Without warning, like a firecracker exploding among the fireworks, a massive detonation crashed out. A vast funnel-shaped mass of black smoke shot out of the car park entrance and billowed into the road. The roar belted out and windows opposite shattered. Bits and pieces of debris showered up and out like grit from a furnace chimney.

The black car immediately started up and pulled away. In moments it was out of sight.

Volumes of black smoke continued to pour from the entrance to the underground car park.

In keeping with his image Peter Crabbe rented a high-class apartment, all bright paintwork and teak veneer and heavy drapes and thick carpets. The spare room contained a mattress and on this the unconscious body of Ray Doyle was hurled down like a sack of potatoes. Crabbe gave a little grunt as he stood back and stared with some resentment at Arthur Pendle.

'Reckon he's hurt bad?' Pendle wanted to know.

'I don't know. Get something to tie him up with.'

73

With Pendle out of the way Crabbe got down to searching through the clothes of the unconscious man. His tough face grew grimmer with his discoveries. There was the gun, a Browning auto, which he looked at, sucking in his cheeks, and then depositing carefully on the floor. There was a driving licence – Raymond Doyle – and an ID Card. At this Crabbe stared with undisguised hatred and anger. When Pendle returned with the length of rope he saw the gun at once.

'I knew he was a cop.'

'Well,' Crabbe said irritably. 'He isn't.'

At Pendle's surprised stare Crabbe simply collected up Doyle's belongings and said: 'Tie him up.'

'Who is he then?'

'Just do as I say.'

Crabbe went out with that hard look which indicated that he was in a mood, and he left Arthur Pendle a sorely puzzled young tearaway.

The long low red brick house dozed serenely in the well-tended garden. Bodie slewed his car into the kerb and fairly charged up to the front door. When the daughter of the house opened he barged in, yelling.

'Forrest! Forrest!'

He blundered across the hall and flung open the door to the living-room, scanned it – empty – went on to the next door, flung that open wide. 'Forrest! I know you're here! Come out before I smash the place apart – get out here now!'

At the top of the stairs Brian Forrest appeared. He was perfectly composed. His small, shrewd face with that down-curved vee of a mouth pursed up at the antics of this boor in his house.

'What the hell do you think you're doing? Who are you?' Madge Forrest and her daughter Carol clustered at the foot of the stairs. 'Carol, phone the police.'

'You so much as touch that phone,' Bodie told the young lady, 'and I'll rip it out.'

Madge Forrest clutched her husband's arm as he reached the hall. 'Brian – don't argue with him!'

'Leave him to me, Madge.' Forrest spoke with the tone of voice of a man accustomed to being obeyed.

'I want to talk to you,' said Bodie. 'And I want the truth – understand?'

'Very well.' As Forrest spoke Bodie caught the unwelcome notion that the man was humouring him. 'What do you want to discuss?'

'There's a girl I know – she's on the critical list. Two people dead and ten others seriously injured. Let's start with them.'

'You're referring to the bombing. How am I supposed to be able to help?'

'That bomb was intended for you. The second one today proves it – and you knew it was coming.' Forrest walked away as Bodie spoke, going into the living-room. He poured a drink at the bar before the lavish bottle display, all a glitter of colour and glass, and Bodie refused a drink. Bodie plugged on. 'For someone who's just escaped death you're pretty cool.'

Holding his drink, Forrest turned back to Bodie. He wore a grey suit and looked smooth and prosperous. His small face was shrewd and alive. There was a bald patch on the crown of his head; but he was alert and fit. 'You want to know what is my connection with these bombings? The answer's very simple. I don't know. I'm an accountant. I've been an accountant all my life. The only injury I can possibly have done anyone is to have overestimated their tax liability – that's hardly a motive for murder, I think you'll agree.' Forrest remained very cheerful.

Bodie glared at him. 'You're ice-cold, Forrest. Anyone else in your position'd be confused, frightened –'

'Why? I told you, I'm an accountant. Accountants are very logical people. What are you?'

Bodie ignored that. 'There have been two attempts on your life and since I've been on your tail, there's some interested party following me, so let's forget this "why" and this "I'm just an accountant" waffle, and talk.'

Forrest flung up his arms in mock despair, the glass glittering high. 'What can I say? You tell me.'

'All right, start by telling me how you were able to set up your business so quickly. Your contacts after you got back from the States – who were they?'

'People I knew, people I'd met. There's no secret about them. If I knew what you were getting at, maybe I could help, but, as it is . . . '

Bodie took a breath. This fellow was getting to him. 'You're lying, Forrest.'

Abruptly the accountant vanished. Angrily, Forrest shouted: 'Don't you call me a liar!'

'You're quite unreal!' Bodie had to fight his own anger. 'You know that? You're unreal! Someone plants a bomb in your car. God knows how you escape getting killed. What's your first reaction? Do you phone the police? Do you even bother to wait for them? No. You just make your way home, pour yourself a scotch, kiss your wife and act like nothing's happened.'

'I was intending to contact the police.'

'When? Next year?'

'It all happened too quickly. I suppose I panicked. My first thought was to get home – '

'You,' Bodie burst out, 'are a bloody liar!'

Madge Forrest came into the room swiftly. Carol had phoned the police, and they were here, and by the sound of it only just in time. She hurried towards her husband as the uniformed men entered.

'Brian!'

Bodie saw – he saw the blue uniforms, and he groaned. He could explain and sort this little lot out; but it would take time. All the way back to CI5 H.Q. he drove in a fuming rage, embittered, frustrated. Forrest had run rings around him, made a monkey out of him. And, now it was George Cowley's turn to drive a few pointed barbs into him. Cowley started off in fine style the moment Bodie was in his office.

'You damned fool.'

Bodie felt too injured to reply to this.

'I warned you.'

Bodie sat silently.

'I could have you for this.'

And Bodie knew this was so. Cowley heaved up a sigh, for he found the scene abruptly distasteful. Then Bodie looked straight at the chief and, very quietly, said: 'I'm right, though. About Forrest.'

'I'm not interested in your opinions.' Cowley shook his head and limped across his office to turn and glare at Bodie. 'You're a good team, you and Doyle. I don't want to lose either of you, if I can help it.'

Bodie put on a doleful look. 'I'm sorry, sir.'

Very briskly, Cowley said: 'Like hell you are.'

Digesting the welcome change in the atmosphere, Bodie handed across the slip of paper bearing the number of the black car. 'Registration number of whoever's been keeping tabs on me.'

Cowley took the slip. The number would be checked out. Then he said in an altogether different tone of voice: 'By the way, your young lady friend – there's some improvement.'

'Thanks.' Bodie couldn't find it in him to add to that.

'Just remember,' Cowley told him, and the steel was back in the plummy voice. 'You disobey any instruction of mine again!' And, soberly listening, Bodie knew the chief meant it. 'Now, I suppose you'd better finish off what you got yourself into in the first place!'

'What about Doyle? What's he come up with?'

'I don't know.' Cowley put a hand down to rub his gammy leg. The damned bullet gave him hell from time to time. 'I haven't heard from him.'

Ray Doyle opened bleary blue eyes and winced as the pain clawed at him. He remembered – the flowers and the scrub and the junk above him, and the sky under him, and an almighty thump in his side . . . That blasted car, creeping up on him, ramming him like a runaway tank ... Gradually he came to. It was a painful process. He was tied up. Automatically he struggled against his bonds and Arthur Pendle's gloating voice said: 'I wouldn't bother.'

Doyle took in the bare room, the mattress, and Pendle's voice.

'Don't bother to shout. No one'll hear you – and you'll get a hell of a headache, too – from me.'

Pendle closed the door and went off to Crabbe's luxuriously appointed kitchen. This was one swell apartment, and he heard the radio muted through the door, the newscaster reading reports of all the mayhem the wide world over. Pendle licked his lips. Well, he was into the mayhem, now, and he liked it. Liked the feel of it.

The newscaster went on to report the carpark bombing, and he said the restaurant bombing was connected. Pendle smirked. Smart! Then: 'The police have issued a photograph and description of a man they wish to interview in connection with the two explosions. He has been named as Arthur Brian Pendle, alias Gary – ' Pendle listened to no more but walked straight to the radio in the plush living-room and switched it off. He was shaking and livid.

Peter Crabbe, enjoying himself in the kitchen opening delicious sounding tins of food for the meal he intended to cordon bleu for himself, heard the newsreport and stood bolt upright. When the radio snapped off he drew a deep, savage breath. His tough face with the blue chin would have frightened a white shark. He went through into the living-room – fast. Pendle still stood by the radio. Crabbe pushed past and switched it on again.

'. . . and of slim build. News is coming in of an airline – '

Crabbe switched off the radio. He was controlling himself; but he was ready to burst out in white-hot fury. 'So they do know who you are. How?'

'They don't!'

'Arthur Brian Pendle – ' Crabbe didn't have to spell it out.

'They don't! They're lying!'

'Alias Gary – Gary who?'

'I've never been copped. I swear it.' Pendle's thin face showed a dim understanding of the fury in Crabbe. He backed off.

'Don't lie! I set it up and you blow it! No form! I fell right in it.'

Defensively, truculently, Pendle said: 'I've done a bit. Everybody's done a bit.'

'You've done enough.' Crabbe felt the blood pounding at his temples. 'You know who we've got in there? Only a CI5 man. Top of the tree, that's all!'

Arthur Pendle swallowed. This was mayhem that grew bigger than he liked. 'What are we going to do with him?'

'Well, we're not going to turn him loose in Piccadilly, that's for sure.'

The phone rang and Crabbe, after a stare at Pendle that would have frizzled armour-plate, answered. It was Phipps.

'What went wrong this time?' demanded Phipps. He was being ridden by Macneil and he didn't like it, not at all. Two bombs, and nothing. Maybe they did need an air raid, at that.

'We'll get him,' said Crabbe.

'I hope so.' In the neat and inconspicuous hotel room Phipps glanced across at Macneil. The American was beginning to reveal something of the murderous ruthlessness that had brought him to his present position. 'My client's getting restless – handing out contracts which aren't fulfilled.' Phipps spoke curtly now. 'This boy you used – get rid of him.'

Listening, Crabbe looked at Pendle. Pendle's tight face glared back, and the killer eyes looked milky with madness.

'I'll take care of it . . .'

Crabbe put the phone down and then checked that Doyle was still safely tied up. Pendle appeared, looking into the room past his shoulder.

'I'm going out for a while,' said Crabbe, abruptly.

'What about – ?'

'I'll handle it. You just say put.'

Crabbe gave Pendle a meaningful look and then went out. Pendle stood for a moment in thought. The mayhem was much nearer than before, no doubt of it.

The long low luxurious home of the Forrests was subjected to another visitor. George Cowley smiled his genial smile as Carol answered the door and Mrs Forrest appeared at her shoulder.

'Mrs Forrest? My name's Cowley. I believe one of my men has been making a nuisance of himself?'

'Oh, yes – '

'I really can't apologise enough. There are, however, a few small points I just need to clarify.'

'Of course,' said Madge Forrest, and she stepped back to allow this polite and friendly gentleman to enter. She was due an apology for the absolutely boorish behaviour of that awful Bodie. In the living-room Cowley remarked upon the charming house and Madge Forrest said thank you and Cowley asked after her husband and she said he'd just popped out to the shops, and they were getting on like a house on fire. Cowley admired the garden, and smiled through the window, and admired the big bowl of roses, pink and red, on a coffee table. Then he said, out of nowhere: 'I understand your husband didn't do National Service?'

Madge Forrest gave a little self-conscious laugh. The switch in conversation was so strange.

'No,' she said. 'He failed his medical. He had asthma as a boy so they wouldn't take him.'

'Really?' Cowley still smiled in his friendly way, the lined face like a friendly Santa Claus. 'That's odd.'

'Odd?'

'Well, because there's no record of his ever having attended a medical.'

Madge Forrest felt confused. This was so strange. 'I don't understand. I'm – I'm not quite with you.'

'We checked. There's definitely no record.'

'Well, I – I suppose it could have got lost.'

Cowley beamed at her. 'I expect so . . .'

He wandered across to the roses and gently partook of their aroma. 'Are these out of your own garden? Beautiful. I do love roses.'

'Mr er – Cowley – was there any particular reason why you asked that question?'

'About your husband you mean? No, no . . . Just a matter of interest.' His smile was still faultless. 'As you say, it probably got lost – along with all his other records.'

The puzzlement in Madge Forrest was turning to alarm. This was odd, very odd . . . 'I beg your pardon?' She felt most uneasy.

'Well, you know how one thing can lead to another. He was born in Jersey. Am I right?'

'That's correct, yes.'

'Except that there are no records to that effect – not even a birth certificate. Indeed, there's no evidence he's even been to the Channel Isles, let alone being brought up there. Neither is there any evidence that his father ever served in the Army, that he was ever issued with a ration book, or that he even existed. There's no record of his parents' death in a car crash, and the English Speaking Union say that no one bearing your husband's name was ever awarded one of their scholarships to go and study in the States.' Cowley's smile had dissipated as he spoke. His words fell like hard pellets, each revealed fact striking at Mrs Forrest, penetrating her armour of complacent good-living. She was dumbstruck.

Cowley went on and the irony fitted exactly. 'As I said, there were just one or two small points I was hoping you could clear up.'

Madge Forrest put out an unsteady hand and found the arm of the deeply-upholstered armchair. Her knees gave way. She sank down. She couldn't think for the roaring in her head, words, phrases, outrageous ideas. Her husband didn't exist! But – but – She wondered if she could have imagined Brian into existence. Like in one of those weird novels she always refused to get out of the library. She put her face into her hands. The world, for Madge Forrest, had turned upside down.

Bodie's dogged surveillance of the infuriating Mr Brian Forrest had paid off handsomely at last. Big dividends. Bodie sat at the wheel of his Capri parked diagonally across from Forrest's second car as the man spoke heatedly to two hard, squarely-built, tough looking men. They had no idea Bodie was watching them. The small sidestreet contained just enough traffic to conceal him – but the passing cars and people could not conceal the car belonging to the two hard cases.

It was a black Triumph.

Bodie licked his lips.

A heated argument was going on over there. The two men were in their thirties and were usefully built. Their clothes were such as to make a Savile Row man wish to vomit. Bodie owed them. Finally, with an angry gesticulation from Forrest to help them on their way, the two men climbed into the black car and drove off.

Bodie let a small and not very pleasant smile disfigure those mobile lips of his. Then he started up and followed gently.

Out on those anonymous concrete ribbons of road running between tree-lined fields and discreet housing estates, Bodie fed the soup to his Capri and roared up alongside the black car. For a long moment the two cars pelted side by side.

Bodie stared across the wind-rushing gap. The moment of recognition passed. As though tired of the game, Bodie roared out ahead, hurtling away from the Triumph. The two men's faces registered shock and then anger and then furious determination. The black car zoomed off in chase.

The two cars pelted along the road. The tail on the kite . . . This time Bodie intended to do it differently, do it right – and if necessary do it for keeps.

He drove with his vision taking in the unwinding road ahead and the speeding black car in the rear-view mirror. They swirled around corners and hared along the road, and Bodie kept his speed just right to infuriate the two men in the pursuing car and make sure they tailed him at the distance he wanted.

Trees, hedgerows, telephone boxes, pubs, wooden gates, all whistled past in a multi- coloured blur.

Bodie kept checking the back straight. A yellow car made a half-hearted attempt to follow on in the procession; but when the black Triumph pursued the silver-grey Capri madly through a narrow railway tunnel, the yellow car gave up in disgust.

When and only when the back road was clear of all other vehicles bar the pursuing black Triumph, Bodie made his move.

The choicest turning appeared ahead, a blind left-hand corner which could be taken at speed by a skilful driver, The man at the wheel of the black car was skilful, Bodie would give the fellow that.

He swung the Capri around with a superb sliding panache of screaming tyres and smoking rubber, hurled the Capri into the second turning that conveniently appeared, slewing the car in a skidding halt that ended up diagonally across the road. Bodie's lips bore that little wrinkle of pleasure that Doyle called diabolically malicious ...

The car was still shaking from the application of the brakes as Bodie bundled out and went headlong over the bonnet to the far side, rolling over and over into the grass.

He was only just in time.

The black Triumph swerved around the corner with screeching tyres. The driver was intent on catching the Capri.

He found the Capri.

The car was parked diagonally across the narrow road directly in his path. Dangerous. Deadly. The steering wheel spun savagely in his hands and the Triumph skidded wildly.

The brakes clamped. But the onward impetus was far too great to stop in the distance.

The black car howled screeching across the road, went up on to the grassy bank, splintered through one white-painted wooden gate, went plunging on like a galleon in a heavy sea, crashed headlong through a second white-painted fence and so dipped down into the field, shuddering, shaking, finally coming to an exhausted rest.

Bodie was over the ruined fence and at the driving side of the Triumph in a few racing strides.

He bore a look of pleased and vengeful anticipation.

He checked the pulses of the two men inside. They were not dead. They were dazed, and blood oozed on the forehead of the driver. Bodie plunged his eager hand inside the jacket. He hauled out a gun, a workmanlike Smith and Wesson .357 Magnum. Then a passport – the size and the green cover told him it was American quite apart from the gold stamping. Then an ID card.

Bodie flicked it open.

Now to find out who these kite-chasing gentlemen were . . .

He looked. The look of amazement and chagrin would have made Cowley and Doyle guffaw.

'Bloody hell!' said Bodie. 'F.B.I.!'

Chapter Six

Wheels within wheels . . . Left hand and right hand . . .
Only, this time, it was Nation not speaking unto Nation . . .

'We should,' said George Cowley with emphasis, 'have
been informed.' He'd said that before and, given the nature
of covert operations, would no doubt say it again. 'I don't
care what the Home Office or your people say.'

The outpatients department of the hospital had just
about finished patching up the two F.B.I. operatives. One
– the driver, Braddock – wore sticking plaster on his forehead over the cut. The other winced every now and again
as he moved his hefty shoulders inside the tweed jacket.
This was Haskell. They were partners, and they were only
too well aware that this Limey CI5 man had made real
monkeys out of them.

Braddock said: 'Our orders were to get Forrest out from
under and fly straight back to the States.'

Both Americans wore their shirt collars unfastened and
their ties pulled down. This added to their dishevelled
look.

'Get Forrest out,' said Cowley, 'from under what?'

'He's an ex-Mafia accountant. Twenty years ago we put
the finger on him. He turned State's Evidence provided we
set him up with a new identity. Change of face, change of
scene.'

Bodie said: 'And the Mob traced him to here – after all this time?'

'Those guys have long memories. They never close the book.'

Braddock's partner, Haskell chipped in. 'You know what they say. Once a crook, always a crook. Well, Forrest's been dabbling over here and that wasn't very smart. Like it or not, the Mob's here, too.'

'Forrest got into a land deal,' amplified Braddock. 'With an American company. But he didn't know he was dealing with a group fronting for the Boys. Their attorney turned out to be a guy Forrest worked with way back.'

Cowley rubbed his leg. His face remained grim. 'So? Don't tell me the F.B.I. provides an After-Care Service for informers!'

Haskell said: 'Forest called us and offered another trade for another new identity. He gives us evidence tying the company with the Mob – and we give him a new cover.'

'Not,' commented Cowley, 'exactly ethical. But practical.'

Bodie butted in. 'Until the bombs started flying.'

'All right.' Cowley made up his mind. He said to the F.B.I. agents: 'You want your evidence, fair enough. But – I want those bombers . . .'

Every movement Ray Doyle made caused him excruciating pain. But he had to be up and doing. This Pendle was a nutter, a real right raving maniac of a nutter. The spare room was furnished well enough for occasional occupancy, and the red telephone squatted on a side table, connected to the outside world. The table and the phone were on the other side of the room. They were almost on the other side of the moon as far as Ray Doyle's mobility was concerned.

But he had to try.

In the expensively-furnished living-room of Peter Crabbe's apartment Arthur Pendle fingered Doyle's Browning auto as though it was a sacred object deserving of worship. Guns! Now Pendle *knew* he was in the big time. Bombs made a satisfying bang and killed people; but they lacked the personal feeling craved by Arthur Pendle. His pale killer eyes leeched on to the blued metal of the automatic and his hands fondled it caressingly.

The door opened and the muted sound of voices in the hall followed by the slam of the front door made Pendle hastily shove the gun away in the table drawer. He slammed the drawer shut and then hopped into an armchair facing the television. Sound and colour were booming and glowing away; but his eyes were filled with the sight of the automatic and his ears with the crackling staccato of shots she'd make if he loosed her off . . .

Peter Crabbe, walked into the living-room, smiling, expansive, ushering his guest in. The two men entered. Crabbe made a small, self-satisfied gesture towards his companion, speaking with dry emphasis introducing Arthur Pendle.

'Arthur. Mr Forrest.'

Arthur Pendle sat frozen in the armchair, gazing in total disbelief at Brian Forrest, whose shrewd small face bore an amused smile.

At that moment as Arthur Pendle stared disbelievingly, Ray Doyle in the spare room toppled his pain-wracked body off the mattress. When he hit he felt as though his ribs had been pushed together like a concertina. His mouth clamped. He did not yell out. He lay there for a moment until the pain-mists cleared, and then he began a dogged, crippled, merciless crawl towards the side table and the red telephone.

Peter Crabbe stared with open amusement at Pendle's expression of dazed disbelief.

'Make yourself at home, Brian,' he said to Forrest. 'Drink?'

'Wouldn't mind,' said Forrest, still looking at Pendle.

Arthur Pendle swallowed and at last found his voice.

'I don't get it. We've been hired to kill you.'

Forrest nodded coolly. 'That's right.'

Crossing to the drinks cabinet, Crabbe switched off the TV. He smiled with self-satisfaction. 'Why,' he said, 'do you think we haven't been successful?'

He poured a large scotch and handed it to Forrest. Pendle looked at the pair of them. 'I still don't get it. When Phipps and his client find out – '

'Don't worry,' Crabbe told him confidently. 'We'll be abroad by then. Brian'll be joining us soon as he's sorted out his insurance.'

'Insurance?'

Forrest swallowed a sip of scotch. 'A couple of men have promised to organise it for me – in return for a few documents.'

As the men in the living-room spoke together, Doyle inched his agonised way across the carpet towards the phone. This was worse than scaling Mount Everest. He paused. He had to get his strength together for the next step, and he felt awful. His face was sheened in sweat. It looked blue and green, shiny. He closed his eyes and took a breath. The breath was more like a desperate gulp. Then he started in on getting the phone off the table and down where he could use it.

Crabbe was asking Forrest: 'What happens to your family?'

'Start another one! who knows . . . ' He took a drink, considering. 'No. No, they'll be all right. I've provided for them.'

'That easy?' Crabbe was fascinated by a man who could shed one identity like a snake skin.

'What can I do? I'll call them once in a while – perhaps. Matter of fact, I must call them now. Where's the phone?'

Forrest crossed to the table at Crabbe's directing nod and picked up the receiver. He put his drink down and started to dial out.

In the spare room Doyle clenched his teeth on the phone cord. He jerked his head back. The red phone moved a fraction and tilted, then flopped back. Again, Doyle hauled on the flex with his powerful jaw muscles locked, his teeth biting in.

Forrest put the phone down in disgust, the beep-beep telling him exactly what his daughter Carol was doing.

'That daughter of mine – she lives on the telephone.'

It was not his daughter Carol on the phone but his wife, Madge. She replaced the receiver. Her face was still drawn, and the shock she had experienced lived like a coiled wire within her. 'He's not at the office,' she said, and sighed, feeling lost.

Carol was reading a magazine curled up on the settee. 'So he's on the way home. What are you worrying about. He's not out on the town! That'd be the day – if he was.'

Madge Forrest's sensation of lost loneliness, the fears she could not explain, the horror of what lay ahead, coalesced into a sob of anguish. 'Those bombs – they were meant for him.'

Carol, the smooth tennis-girl whose horizons were bound by girl-friends' gossip and potential boy-friends, looked up from her magazine. 'What?' Something was wrong with her mother. 'But you said it was all a mistake. You said Mr Cowley told you it was all a mistake.'

'I told you a lie.' Madge Forrest's voice threatened to crack with the turmoil torturing her. 'But your father has been lying to me all our married life. I – we, don't really know anything about him.'

'But he's just – I mean, he's Dad, plain old nine-to-five Daddy. There's no mystery about him.'

'I wish he were. It's funny. There were times when I longed for a bit of excitement, for something to happen, to liven us up a bit instead of being shut up in this – this wall-to-wall, roses-round-the-door time capsule. Now it has happened and I'm frightened. I'm very frightened . . .'

'Mummy!' Carol was now alarmed. She stood up and walked across to her mother. She put her arms around her shoulders. 'Any minute now, he's going to walk in the door. Have his nightly scotch and soda and bury his head in *The Financial Times*.'

Madge put up a hand and clasped her daughter's hand on her shoulder. Her voice whispered hoarsely. 'I don't think so.'

Doyle's teeth gripped on to the telephone flex like a bull-dog's teeth into the pants of the stage comic. He pulled. He pulled so that the blood thundered in his head and he felt his eyeballs were starting out on stalks. The red telephone tilted, tilted again, overbalanced. It fell full on to his chest. He let go of the cord and expelled his breath in a whoosh. His chest proved to be a capital landing zone for red telephones. He wriggled around, tilted the phone off, got his bound hands around and twisted up so he could feel the holes in the dial and count around. Laboriously, doggedly, Ray Doyle started to dial out CI5 H.Q.

The ringing tone burred from the receiver. Hastily, Doyle wriggled himself around on the carpet, feeling his injuries driving white-hot splinters of pain into his abused body.

'Come on,' he said. 'Come on.'

The ringing stopped and a girl's voice said: 'CI5. Major Cowley's office –'

As loud as he dared, his mouth stuck right into the telephone mouthpiece, Doyle said: 'It's Ray Doyle. Four five! Get a trace on this number as quick as you can. Tell Cowley –'

The girl's voice floated tinnily up from the receiver.

'I'm sorry. I can hardly hear you.'

Doyle choked back a groan of despair. Sweat stung his eyes. His curly mop of hair stood out like a chimney-sweep's brush. He felt lousy. His face was smothered in sweat and lumped with bruises to add to the bump under his right eye. He swallowed down and started in repeating the message.

Out in the living-room Forrest was speaking with an odd note in his voice that Crabbe could not identify. 'I'll miss the girl,' Forrest said, rolling his whisky glass between his palms. 'But I'm not sure I'll be sorry to trade Madge in for a new model!'

'She helped give you a respectable front,' Crabbe pointed out.

'Yes. I'll try phoning again.' He picked up the phone

again and listened. His face looked puzzled. He couldn't quite make out what was going on. 'Funny . . .'

A single startled glance flung between Crabbe and Pendle told each what was wrong. Crabbe started to his feet; but Pendle, running like a wildman, was already crossing the living-room. He ran out the door towards the spare room.

Forrest stared for a moment. Then he hastened out after Crabbe who was running full tilt after Arthur Pendle.

Pendle burst into the spare room.

He fairly flung himself on the prostrate Doyle, tearing the phone away and hurling it on to the floor. Pendle's face was hysterically contorted. His killer's eyes were so pale they appeared mere hollow spaces. He started kicking and punching at Doyle, who tried to protect his vitals, but the very vehemence of Pendle's actions precluded accurate attack.

Then Crabbe appeared and tried to drag Pendle away, yelling.

'Arthur! No!'

Pendle was screaming and thrashing and the appalled Forrest, standing in the door, was perfectly assured that the young tearaway would, indeed, kill the man with his wrists tied.

Finally Crabbe contrived to haul Pendle away and got him out of the spare room. Forrest followed, shaken. Crabbe threw Pendle down on to the sofa where he shouted at him, shook his fist, managed to get some control back into the killer's brain. Pendle shook. Suddenly, he folded up, hugging his stomach in the blue jersey, and a laxness descended on him as though, very suddenly, he had run out of breath.

Forrest felt it was time to re-assert his authority.

'What's going on? You didn't tell me —'

'He'll be all right.'

'All right?' Forrest's face expressed distaste. 'What the hell's the matter with him?'

'Nothing!' Crabbe sensed the danger in this for him, personally. 'Nothing's the matter.'

'You call that nothing? He's a maniac!'

'He's all right. I can handle it.'

Forrest looked down on Pendle, who had obviously calmed down considerably. He slumped there, dejected. Unsure what to do or say, feeling the pressures on him that he habitually shrugged off, he went back to the spare room. Whoever that was in there ...

He went in and stared thoughtfully at the bound and huddled figure on the floor. He saw the red telephone receiver lying on the floor. He was aware of the piercing blue eyes watching him as the man stirred and, as Forrest realised, despite himself uttered a groan of pain.

Deliberately, Forrest jerked the flex away, threw the severed end down over the phone.

Then he went back to the living-room. Being an accountant gave you habit-forming ideas of neatness.

Pendle had slunk off into one of the bedrooms. He closed the door behind him. Crabbe glanced up wearily as Forrest came back into the living-room.

The tone of voice sparked up as Forrest demanded: 'That man in there? Who is he?'

Easily, forcing his tough smile to work for him, Crabbe said: 'Turned out quite handy, really. When I blow this place sky high the police'll think it's my body they've found in the wreckage.'

At this Forrest began to look worried.

'But who *is* he?'

'CI5.'

Forrest felt the breeze pass over his forehead. He felt the blood thump in his heart.

'Cop killing! On top of everything else.'

'That everything else you mention has lined our pockets for a long time to come.'

Forrest made a gesture with his hand as though to say that was to come, and this CI5 man was here and now.

And there were other problems Forrest could see in the here and now.

'Young Pendle. How big is his share?'

Crabbe looked at Forrest. 'Incredible. You really are. The ramrod straight city gent. Even I'd buy a used car from you . . . Not that you'd dabble in anything so lowly. And, you're more ruthless than anyone.'

'Practical.' Forrest spoke briskly, getting his self-possession back. 'More practical. That's all. I asked you about Pendle.'

Peter Crabbe smiled. The smile was not pleasant, and it told Brian Forrest all he needed to know.

But Crabbe added, meaningfully: 'The police might find two bodies . . .'

Chapter Seven

The offices of Forrest and Padgett looked as though a herd
of rampaging elephants had trampled all over them. But
these elephants knew exactly what they were doing. As
Bodie and the F.B.I. agent Haskell turned the office upside
down under Cowley's directions, the other F.B.I. operative,
Braddock, stood before the wall safe. His practised fingers
twirled the knob and he listened to the tumblers with the
pleased smile of a man who knows he is winning at roulette.

Richard Padgett, stout, perspiring, flustered, smoothed
his silver hair and yelped his outrage at Cowley.

'It's outrageous! Outrageous! Those are all confidential
papers!'

'If I were you, Dick,' Cowley advised the florid-faced
man with a quietness that concealed nothing of his meaning. 'I should stop worrying about any of this and start
looking for a new partner.'

As Padgett digested that unwelcome information, with a
sliding click the wall safe opened. Braddock delved inside
like a magician into a top hat, and the rabbits he brought
out, in the shape of bulky files and papers, were at once
pounced on by Bodie.

As Cowley stepped forward to join him, the phone rang,
and Padgett, answering, sighed and indicated the call was

for Cowley. The CI5 chief answered as Bodie, riffling through the papers, came up with one that caught his immediate attention.

'Carrick Holdings,' Bodie read. 'Directors: Brian Forrest... Peter Crabbe...'

Padgett said: 'Carrick? I've never heard any mention of that.'

On the phone Cowley had given someone a piece of his mind and now he said, with that bark of command in his voice that brooked no nonsense: 'Right! Give it to me.'

Bodie tapped the paper in his hand musingly. 'Peter Crabbe...'

'You know him?' Haskell still looked pale about the gills, but F.B.I. and CI5 had shaken hands and made it up.

'He's involved in one of the big protection rackets,' Bodie told Haskell. 'But he's always several moves away from the action.'

Cowley put the phone down. 'Not this time. The call was traced. That's where Doyle was calling from. No wonder the contract missed the target. Your mobsters,' he said, half turning to the F.B.I. operatives, 'gave the contract to kill Forrest to Forrest's partner.'

Bodie ignored the mottled look about Padgett that suggested he was going to have a stroke at any minute.

'So Forrest fooled you – and the Mafia. They must want to see Crabbe as much as we do.'

Haskell cooed: 'I like it.' He stared at his partner, elated. 'I like it.'

Brusquely, leading the way out, Cowley commented: 'There's no accounting for taste.'

Peter Crabbe had organised it all with the loving care that had brought him to his present successful position. Protection meant what it said. He had started when he had discovered the salutary effects of even a small bomb on the fragile economy of a small shop. Bombs fascinated him. For this one, the one that would blow his expensive and

95

luxurious penthouse apartment to smithereens, he had spent a deal of effort and thought.

The CI5 man would be sent off in fine style.

He checked over the bomb – the explosive device – for the last time. He clicked his tongue against his teeth, satisfied.

He turned to Pendle, who was watching with his cheeks sucked in.

'While we're taking the stuff down to the car, untie him and bring him in here. Lay him about three feet away from the charge. No nearer.'

Pendle nodded and, with a last look at the bomb, went towards the door of the living-room. Crabbe and Forrest collected up the suitcases to be taken down to the car park. Pendle had recovered his poise – his cool. As he went into the spare room he unlimbered his knife. The knife had served him well before now; but this day had brought him a new and much greater toy. He licked his lips and bent over Doyle.

Doyle's blue eyes regarded the tearaway as though the knife was to be used for real. But, a sly smile disfiguring his narrow face, Pendle sliced through the rope binding legs to wrists. Doyle's body flopped open like a broken-backed book. Pendle cut the ropes binding his ankles.

'Right. In the other room . . . ' As Pendle reached down a hand, Doyle tried to move. The process was painful and felt to him like his feet and legs had been dipped in acid. Pendle gave him a push and, perforce, Doyle half-staggered, half-fell out of the door. With a deal of difficulty, Pendle manoeuvred Doyle over to the explosive device. He wasn't too finicky about the three feet distance Crabbe had stipulated.

Doyle collapsed on the floor, his legs, although returning to life, feeling more like columns of jelly than human legs.

Pendle took out Doyle's gun.

The blood flowing again in Doyle's legs brought strength as well as agony. He was no good as a CI5 man with legs made of jelly . . .

Arthur Pendle fondled the Browning auto. He knelt down beside Doyle, quite slowly, savouring every moment of his sadistic act. He pointed the muzzle at Doyle's temple.

'Recognise it? 'Cos it's yours.' He licked his lips again, relishing every moment. 'Except now it's mine.'

With a shuddery recogntion of what was to come next, Doyle saw Pendle swivel the gun and lift it high. The butt would come crashing down in the next instant. It would be lights out for Ray Doyle, lights out for good, for he had not missed the significance of the device on the floor. Bombs – they were to be used to finish off the business as they had begun it. The gun lifted. Pendle's eyes held that milky look of killing madness. He might easily crush Doyle's skull through with the butt and not give a damn . . .

Doyle used those jelly-legs of his. He kicked out with all the strength he could find. A great gasp of explosive effort burst past his lips. He kicked Arthur Pendle just as the killer swung the gun down and Pendle went toppling over off balance. His head crunched into the leg of the table. The gun flew up in the air and curved away to crash down with a heavy thud on the carpet beyond the table.

Doyle took a whooping breath and rolled himself as fast as he could through the door into the kitchen. He kicked the door shut after him on the sight of Pendle wriggling around like a worm on a hook. Doyle had a few moments, a few moments only . . .

He spotted the cupboard standing alongside the kitchen door. If that was screwed to the wall . . . With an effort that sapped his strength he staggered up. He leaned against the end of the cupboard, fighting for breath, gulping air, feeling the sweat stinking all over his body, struggling to find the strength.

Then, with a convulsive unspringing of his muscular body he heaved against the cupboard.

The pain gripped him as he thrust. He didn't yell out, for his teeth were clamped, but it felt as though he was yelling the top of his head off.

7.   · 97

The cupboard groaned, moved, a plate fell off, and then the whole thing crashed over in a smother of destruction and lodged up against the door. There'd be no opening that door short of a breaking and entering. Doyle caught a single breath and then, half-turned and looking over his shoulder, hauled out the drawers which flew out on their sides. Tablecloths – then the cutlery, knives and forks and spoons spraying out and clattering all over the floor.

Doyle fell on the cutlery as a starving man falls on bread.

The door shook to a shoulder charge and bashed in against the wedging cupboard. Doyle, scrabbling for a sharp kitchen knife, let a wicked nasty smile cross his abused face.

Arthur Pendle threw himself at the door again, raging, almost foaming, hurling himself insensately at the kitchen door.

With a yell of baulked rage he swung back into the room and stared straight at the tall menacing form of Phipps who had just entered through the opened door. At his side stood a tough-looking man Pendle did not know, a neat and inconspicuous-looking man. On Phipps's other side stood a man who was at once understood by Pendle. This was the heavy, the arm, the protection and the clobberer for the other two.

Phipps said: 'Where's Crabbe?'

Pendle gasped out: 'I don't know, Mr Phipps, I – '

The inconspicuous man spoke in a deep American voice. 'You'd better know, sonny . . .'

Phipps simply motioned to the heavy. He wore clothes that were perfectly ordinary. His shoulders were large and they strained the cloth of his jacket. His hands were large and they reached for Arthur Pendle. His face and features were large, and they expressed a dim and glutinous pleasure in his work.

Pendle yelled and back-pedalled. He was rapidly growing hysterical again. He started to throw small objects from the wall cabinets at the heavy – a cigarette lighter, framed photos – until Phipps circled behind him and gripped his arms. Pendle screamed and struggled and the heavy stepped in and slogged a bunch of fives into his guts. Arthur Pendle became silent.

Phipps stepped back and Pendle slumped. He glanced at Macneil.

The heavy stood back to allow the guv'nors to get on with whatever it was they wanted here. Macneil said dispassionately: 'Get rid of him.'

Pendle's guts were on fire; but he lay on the carpet, winded, and he knew exactly where he was. He could see, appearing tilted on the side, the room and the men moving about searching for something. But Arthur Pendle had fallen by Doyle's abandoned automatic. He gathered himself. His hand closed on the gunbutt.

Phipps and the heavy saw Pendle rising, saw the wicked-looking automatic in his hand, aimed at them, and they saw the maniacal determination to kill screaming from those filmed milky killer's eyes.

Without hesitation Macneil whipped a revolver from his pocket, levelled it at Arthur Pendle, and fired.

The shot slammed Pendle back into the chair, from which, limply, he fell forward and collapsed on the floor.

Doyle heard the shot. He didn't know what was going on, but he sawed with the kitchen knife at his bonds and managed, along with the loss of more skin and blood, to free himself. He looked around for another weapon besides the knife.

Under Macneil's orders the heavy searched through the rooms and found them empty. When he tried the kitchen door it would not budge. At once Macneil crossed to stare at the stubborn door.

'Crabbe?' he said. Then, harshly: 'Break it down.'

The heavy laid those beefy shoulders against the door and it shuddered and rebounded from the blocking cupboard. Again the heavy bashed. He had a great deal more weight and power than Pendle; the door groaned and the cupboard shifted. In seconds now the cupboard would collapse and the door shatter . . .

Phipps added his weight. Both men bashed and thumped at the door. Any second now . . .

Macneil saw that the young tearaway he had shot was no longer in the room. His face suddenly showed more vicious anger than any expression of emotion he'd so far shown in this business that was so messy he just didn't care to think what the boys would say back home.

'The boy – where is he?' The answer obviously lay outside the apartment. 'You get Crabbe. I'll get the boy!' He drew his gun again and started out of the apartment after Pendle.

In the corridor he was just in time to see the wounded boy flop into the elevator. He made a dash for it, the gates slid shut, and Macneil saw the lights start to descend. With a grunt of annoyance he headed for the stairs.

In Crabbe's apartment the battered kitchen door groaned against the resisting cupboard. Doyle, feeling like a wreck abandoned on the Goodwin Sands, looked for the weapon he needed and found it. He swept pots and tins away in a wild smashing and hauled out a satisfying big pepper pot with a screwed lid. He unscrewed the lid and then humped himself back, away from the shuddering, shaking cupboard. The noise erupted through the kitchen and the devils of pain in his head countermarched in hobnailed boots. He shut his eyes, shook his head – a mistake, that – and, gripping the pepperpot firmly, opened his eyes ready for the bastards outside.

The silver-grey Capri howled into the car park and Bodie leaped out, running, belted into the concrete entrance and checked the lifts. One was on its way down. The second stood empty and Bodie whistled in and thumbed the penthouse button. As the lift gates closed, clang-clang, he chuntered through his teeth: 'Come on! Come on!' The lift began to ascend.

The kitchen door was a shred of splintered wood. The cupboard groaned as its jointings split. It rocked and then soughed sideways, spilling the last of the clutter. It collapsed. The door burst inwards . . .

. . . The lift gates opened and Bodie charged out like a rhinoceros. He heard the yelling and bashing and he went bald-headed for the right door. He smashed through into Peter Crabbe's apartment . . .

. . . The cupboard fell away, the kitchen door smashed open, and Doyle, holding himself as straight as he could, fighting the sickening tremble in his limbs, saw the two men rampaging over the wreckage to get at him. With a round-arm swing he hurled the contents of the pepper pot full in their faces.

The pepper settled about them like a cloud of stinging wasps.

They began to shriek and fall about, clutching at their faces, rubbing their eyes, yelling . . .

Bodie waded into them like a rampant sledge-hammer. He hit Phipps flush along the jaw and the man went down, out cold.

The heavy forced his gluey streaming eyes open and traded two punches before Bodie slugged him down unmercifully. The heavy buckled up, hit the wall, collapsed.

Bodie stood back, hardly panting, as Doyle staggered from the kitchen. He held his chest and he wheezed. A few grains of pepper still floated stingingly on the air.

'Dumb – ' Doyle started to say, and choked. He fought for breath. He managed to croak out: 'What took you so long?'

'Shut up!' said Bodie, fiercely. 'You look terrible.'

Doyle ground out: 'Crabbe and Forrest. They're down in the car park. Well, go on!' He was clinging on to the wreckage of the cupboard now, ready to fall down. The sweat on his face coated him like a brazen idol's mask. 'I can't. I'm going to call myself an ambulance.'

Bodie gave his partner a swift searching look. Doyle started to lurch over towards the phone. Bodie thought he'd make it – just. He ran out of the room heading for the lifts and the car park . . .

. . . Arthur Pendle fell out of the lift as it reached the basement level. He started to drag himself out, stumbling to the concrete and crawling along, croaking. He could see Crabbe and Forrest by the car.

Crabbe turned. He saw Pendle. Shocked, he started forward. 'Arthur!'

Crabbe started to run and Pendle tried to stand up to make the last few yards.

Macneil appeared in the entrance from the stairwell. He took in the situation. His gun came up. He fired. Arthur Pendle's body twitched as the slug bit into him. He fell.

Shaken, Crabbe halted by the prostrate body, looked down in horror and then relief. He was vaguely aware of Forrest, in a panic, leaping into the car and driving away. But Crabbe looked down at Pendle. Half musingly, he said: 'Saved me the trouble.'

Macneil simply stepped out of the shadows, revolver lifted, took aim at the exposed and vulnerable form of Crabbe.

Macneil's forefinger whitened on the trigger.

A hand appeared from the side and wrenched the gun away.

A Browning auto was pushed hard against Macneil's temple.

Bodie stepped out. He gave Macneil a look of contempt and then stared at Peter Crabbe, standing, forlorn and abandoned, over the dead body of Arthur Pendle.

The silence in the concrete car park seemed to draw a shroud over the violence, to seal it off, and the gunsmoke fumes in the air quickly dissipated in the ventilation.

In the departures washroom at Heathrow, Forrest was washing up and feeling remarkably happy. Everything had worked out fine. Braddock and Haskell, the F.BI. men who had fixed up a new identity for him, were not the best of company; but he felt secure with them around. They stood in the washroom like rugged sentries with a deal of the rough-haired puppy about them, hardly likeable, but useful.

The tannoy crackled and spat out words just decipher-able.

'British Airways announce the departure of Flight 501 to New York. Passengers should proceed to Gate Nine-teen ...'

'That's us,' said Braddock, moving forward.

Haskell was carefully packing away documents into a briefcase and looking satisfied.

Forrest finished drying his hands. 'Be strange seeing Sydney again, even if it is only a flying visit. You fellows ever been to Australia?'

Forrest didn't give a damn if they had or not. He was going to begin a new life there and he was confident the pickings would be good for a smart operative with the right connections.

Haskell shook his head. 'Can't say I have. You, Orville?'

Braddock did not smile. 'No, sir.'

The mirror behind the washbasins showed two reflec-tions. One was of a sandy-haired man with a lined, hard face that bore strong traces of a warm humanity that could be put aside at certain times. The other reflection was that of a smooth, dark-haired man with mobile lips and, at the moment, down-drawn eyebrows that gave his face a truly Satanic look.

Cowley heard the last bit, about Australia.

He spoke precisely, in his plummy voice.

'You're not going there either, Forrest. We have some-thing else in mind for you.'

The two F.B.I. men remained still. Forrest looked up, the towel draped ridiculously across his hands. His face showed the beginning flicker of the horror ahead.

'A long and very secure stay,' Bodie told him. 'In this country. Very secure and very long. On the moors, prob-ably ...'

The hospital tended to acquire a rush of work when CI5 were in action. Ray Doyle lay in the white bed, half-propped up, feeling that life held all kinds of mysterious and exciting possibilities.

Like the attractive nurse who ministered to him with such grace and such attention. Already the compact of their eyes had suggested great things to come.

The door opened and Bodie entered, manipulating a great sheaf of flowers in their cellophane. His face looked relaxed. He stared at Doyle in the bed. Doyle smirked.

'Oh, you shouldn't have.'

'I didn't,' Bodie told his partner. 'They're for Claire in the other ward.'

'How's she doing?'

'Fine.' Bodie felt that. It added up to a reason for the idiotic stupidities all around. 'Except she's talking of ditching me. Reckons I'm too dangerous to hang around with.'

Doyle did not fail to notice how Bodie's sharp eyes were roving in a most familiar way. His gaze encompassed the shapely form of the young nurse, and the nurse was responding to the approval. Bodie dragged his attention away from the nurse and spoke to Doyle.

'So – how are you feeling?'

'Apart from the ribs or including them?' The bandaging had been very thorough, a Tutankhamen of a job on him. 'Didn't you even bring me any grapes.'

'All those pips?' Bodie tut-tutted. 'Very messy in bed.'

The young nurse left the room with a departing smile of great beauty that favoured both men. Bodie perked up, visibly preening. Doyle frowned.

'Hey! Hands off! She's mine . . . She comes with the tablets . . . '

Chapter Eight

The big hard man in the windcheater and slacks hefted the two-gallon can of petrol as though it was a tin of beans. He looked a hard man, he acted like a hard man, and the effect was heightened by the stocking mask he wore rolled on top of his head. His face was narrow for so big and hard a man, his eyes very bright and knowing. As he poured the petrol over a stack of leaflets in the shadowed yard behind the row of shops he personified ruthlessness.

The grimed bricks of the walls enclosing the yard suddenly bloomed to an orange glow. The flames from the fire leaped and cavorted in the night air, the smoke lifting away to invisibility.

The big man tossed the spent match on to the blaze and stepped back. Two more men appeared, hefty, useful-looking individuals, wearing their stocking masks pulled over their faces. They carried neatly-wrapped bundles of leaflets. One by one, as though aiming each bundle at the heart of the fire, they tossed the leaflets into the flames. Sparks spat and the fire seized greedily upon the paper.

The hard man in the windcheater and slacks gazed for a moment on the flames and their reflections in his eyes gave him the look of a satisfied devil. Then, with a decisive movement, he jerked the stocking mask over his face and re-entered the building.

The shop was small and apeared to have been empty for some time. Stacks of leaflets awaiting distribution were piled on a wooden trestle table. The little platen-printing machine sat inky and silent, and the ink-stained racks gaped like cages from which the pigeons have flown. Men were carrying the leaflets outside to be burned. Two men held a third against the inside wall. They were not gentle with him, and Pellin, an effeminate and inoffensive character, felt his shoulders rick as they shoved him back.

Pellin tried to shake some sense into himself; he had to believe what was happening, and he had to fight the fear tearing at him. But he was not a strong man, and these brutes possessed strength that terrified of itself.

The leader swaggered into the little print-shop and planted himself in front of Pellin.

'We warned you,' he said. He pulled a train ticket from the windcheater pocket and waved it before Pellin's face, almost thrusting it down his gullet. 'One-way ticket, back to your own town. We don't want your kind in our city, Pellin.'

'You're crazy!' Pellin husked. 'All of you. We're perfectly legal. When the police hear of this – '

'The police! Their teeth have been drawn when it comes to dealing with filth like you. But us . . . ? We've still got all our teeth!' The big chest swelled under the shirt beneath the wincheater. 'And we bite!'

The bundles of leaflets were now almost all gone from the trestle table. The flames in the yard illuminated Pellin's face, the starting sweat on his forehead, the tremble to his mouth.

The leader's hard eyes saw all that. He bore on, ruthlessly, hammering his words home.

'Most of us here have got wives . . . kids . . . we want them to grow up in a clean city. That's why we're getting rid of dirt like you.'

Pellin licked his lips and said: 'Run me out?'

'And before we get rid of you we're going to give you a taste of what's waiting for you if you ever come back here again.' His voice rasped out viciously. 'Turn him!'

The bewildered Pellin was efficiently twisted about so that he faced the wall. The two men held him in grips he knew he would never break. He felt the ripping of cloth and the quick breeze of cold over his bare back.

The leader reached down to the big brass buckle of the thick and heavy leather belt around his waist.

'Hold him,' he commanded.

The belt made a sibilant whisper as it slid through the trouser loops.

The neatly-lettered sign in gold leaf on the door read:
G. GREEN O.B.E. – CHIEF CONSTABLE

The chief constable said: 'Come in,' in response to the knock on his door.

Green had once been very tough and the cragginess about his face persisted despite encroaching fat. His body was too fleshy for a fully-active man; but his rat-trap mind was still perfectly capable of running his city. Just past fifty, he felt he had made a success of life and was viewing the prospects to come with a restlessness he hardly understood in himself. Known as a martinet, he got the best out of his men, and regarded himself as firm but just.

He looked up as Inspector Chives entered.

'Ah, Inspector Chives.' He tapped the papers on his desk. 'Glad to see that disgusting organisation decided to pack up and leave.'

'Yes, sir,' said Chives. He no longer wore a windcheater and slacks, and the stocking mask had gone. 'Our city smells a bit cleaner this morning. We won't be seeing Mr Pellin here again.'

George Cowley came out of the inconspicuous back entrance of the building whose ornate frontage sprawled a whole block. He sniffed the evening air. He'd just spent an hour or so explaining the facts of life to the F.B.I. and why Brian Forrest was going to be a guest of Her Majesty. The air smelled good enough to make him decide to walk. He set off, swinging along jauntily, feeling the marvellously free easiness of that damned leg of his. If the surgeons tried to remove the bullet, they had told him gravely, there was no guarantee they could save the leg. Better occasional bouts of excruciating pain than being a peg leg.

He had walked perhaps a block and a half before he was confident that the car idling along over the road was really following him. He crossed over and made a few turns and soon there was no doubt. His face lost its glow of appreciation of a fine evening. If some joker wanted to play fun and games with the chief of CI5, he had, George Cowley reckoned with all due modesty, picked a bad choice.

He reached his own apartment block and sauntered in gently, not hurrying, not dawdling, just taking it nice and easy.

The tailing car stopped smoothly into the kerb and the driver alighted. He hesitated for only a moment and then went swiftly into the block after Cowley.

The foyer was illuminated; but the small lamps cast light across the polished floor and the potted palms and the lift gates and tended to leave the corners and alcoves in shadow. The car driver looked about, saw the stairs, and started for them. He had reached a fluted column supporting the mezzanine and was about to go padding on when a hand reached from the shadows and fastened around his neck like a remora.

In an instant the driver was turned about, thrown down on to the carpet and Cowley was kneeling on him, holding him down in a cunning lock. With a one-armed lift, Cowley hauled him upright and slammed him sharply against the column.

'All right, what's it all about? You've been tailing me — why!'

Cowley's hand frisked the effeminate-looking man with an expertise that Bodie and Doyle would have envied. The wallet flipped open.

Cowley read aloud: 'Thomas Henry Pellin.'

'Yes,' said Pellin. He felt as though his backbone had

been broken through in four places, and the fluted column was doing unmentionable things to his tender skin. 'You are Cowley, aren't you? George Cowley?'

'If I weren't you might have made it. Och, man, I've got eyes in my backside. What's it about?'

'I had to see you, Mr Cowley . . . Talk to you . . . ' The naked entreaty in his words got to Cowley then. 'I should be able to trust *you.*'

Cowley fancied the threat he had envisaged did not exist. He relaxed that ferocious grip by a fraction.

'Trust me?'

'I've read about you. About CI5. Incorruptible.'

'What,' said Cowley, 'the devil are you talking about?'

Pellin sucked in a breath. He was intelligent enough to know when to speak out and he was getting his breath back from the frightening power and devastating speed of this man Cowley.

'Madness,' he said, on a breath. 'Power. Illegal enforcement.'

Cowley absorbed that. This fellow Pellin looked to be the kind of man who would prefer backgammon to sparring as his form of recreation. He let go altogether and stepped back. Pellin rubbed his throat and flexed his arms, wincing as he felt the beginnings of four finger-sized bruises.

'You're pretty good.'

'And you're lucky,' Cowley told him. 'A few years ago and I'd have broken your arm.'

Pellin said: 'You've mellowed?'

And Pellin's sickly face broke into a tentative smile. That got to Cowley. He felt the tension going, felt the way the atmosphere changed, and he guessed his own eyes twinkled.

'My place is on the first floor. Come on . . . '

Pellin moved aside to let Cowley go first. Cowley smiled. He made a small but significant gesture.

'No. You first. I've not mellowed that much!'

George Cowley's flat held that indefinable attribute of

perfect taste. It was masculine and restful, spare, with a few very good antiques to blend with the furnishings. Photographs on the walls and mementoes here and there emphasised Cowley's world-wide travels and the memories he cherished. He crossed to the window and drew the curtains closed and then set about pouring a good dram of pure malt.

He offered a glass to Pellin, indicating the massive Chesterfield and as the young man sat down, thankfully, Cowley brought across the cut-glass sparkling in the lamplight.

'I've just come back, Mr Cowley, and I *know*. Go right through that city, even the suburbs, and there isn't a porno magazine in sight.'

'I can't say I have feelings either way about that.'

'But not just porn – not even a girlie magazine, nothing. But I'm like you, it doesn't bother me either way.'

Cowley sat in his armchair and held his glass, looking up with the furrows across his brow. 'Then why . . . ?'

'That's just the tip of the iceberg.' Pellin went on speaking now in a low, intense voice, looking down at his glass of whisky. 'I'm secretary of the Gay Youth Organisation, Mr Cowley. No, you're right, I am not homosexual myself, but many of my friends are and I've seen them suffer because of bigotry and ignorance. Two weeks ago we opened a branch in that city, just a place where homosexuals could find help and sympathy. It was stopped before it even started.'

'Stopped?'

'Oh, we'd heard whispers about citizens' committees, vigilantes . . . That happens to us in every town. But what happened to us there . . . We were run out. Our H.Q. was wrecked.'

'Who?'

'A bunch of thugs. Masked.' Pellin shivered, suddenly, remembering. He took a gulp of the whisky.

'Well,' pointed out Cowley, briskly but in a friendly way.

110

'That kind of thing can happen. You can't blame a whole city because – '

'I reported it to the police,' broke in Pellin, firmly, now he had reached the crux. 'Told them I had no intention of leaving. They listened, made some noises about making enquiries – and then the thugs came back again, Mr Cowley. This time they gave me a taste ... '

'What?'

'A taste of what I would get if I didn't leave town that night.'

With that Pellin stood up and turned around, putting his drink on the mahogany side table and stripping off his jacket. He pulled up his shirt. Cowley saw the contusions and weals striped all across the white skin, and winced. He knew something about the way men could be beaten, and he did not like what he saw.

Pellin pulled his shirt down and without putting on his jacket flopped back in the sofa. And now Cowley saw why the man hadn't leaned back. 'Just a taste, Mr Cowley.'

'My God! What did the police say about that?'

Pellin shook his head wearily. 'I didn't tell them.'

Cowley looked astonished and opened his mouth; but Pellin went on. 'Mr Cowley, I was alone at the H.Q. – to all intents and purposes it was closed up. Nobody knew I was there. Nobody knew I intended staying on. Nobody – except the police.' Now he looked steadfast at Cowley and his gaze locked with Cowley's. 'No, I didn't tell the police – because I got the terrible feeling that they already knew!'

Cowley's decision to take what Pellin revealed seriously was a part and parcel of the make-up of the chief of CI5. He had been placed in a position of very great power and responsibility and was at all times actually aware of the fact. He did not care, did not care at all, for what had been done to Pellin's back. And if the young man's story was true, it behoved George Cowley to act. But, action must follow thought and planning and that must follow observation and the collection of evidence. Cowley went to see the minister.

The minister, smooth, well-fed, loaded down with his own responsibilities, was better aware than most men of the value of Cowley's CI5. Cowley's Incorruptibles, they were sometimes called, along with the Big A and the Squad.

'The mountain comes to Mohammed,' the minister said, with a pleasant jocularity that did not conceal the tang of real awareness that what he was saying was true.

'It's good of you to see me, sir,' said Cowley in best formal style, his face although pleasant perfectly concealing his little smile.

'I'm curious.' The minister waved the papers. 'Why this sudden interest in a local police force?'

'Local? They control one of the biggest cities in the country and – ' a nasty thought occurred to George Cowley. He eyed the minister. 'You didn't go directly to source!' As the minister regarded him blandly, he said: 'No. No, of course not.'

'I didn't have to go to source, George. This is one police force the Home Office is *acutely* aware of at this time.'

'Why?'

'The example they set. Just three years since Green took over. Gerry Green, the Chief Constable – he began as a very new broom indeed. *And* he's still sweeping exceedingly clean.'

'Impressive – ?'

'Mind blowing.' The minister did look pleased. To have one clean spot in the general murkiness was a beginning in the right direction. 'In just three years he's reduced the crime rate by twenty-two per cent. Arrests and convictions are up by – '

Cowley broke in incredulously. 'Twenty-two per cent! That's unheard of.'

'It's unequalled as far as our records show. Green runs a very tight ship, George.'

'So did Captain Bligh.' Cowley was disturbed and well aware of the slur on Bligh's name; but the image fitted.

112

The minister caught his tone. 'Eh? George – we are not thinking of rocking that ship in any way, are we?'

'I don't know.'

'*George.*'

Abruptly Cowley rounded on the minister. He was aware of the office about him, the impressiveness of the building, the weight of government, the responsibilities, the pressures. And he was aware, too, how attractive short cuts were, how alluring the easy solution.

'Do you trust me?' He spoke with a fierceness that dinted his forehead, and that set the minister a little back on his heels. But the minister was not a politician for nothing.

'Totally, utterly, implicitly. *Up to a point!*'

Cowley spoke flatly now, a hard man setting out a little of what holding to the brief he had been given entailed. 'Not a whisper outside of this office. No inter-departmental communications. I want permission to nose around Green's well-policed city for a while.'

'You're not going to tell me why, of course.'

'Not at the moment – no.' Cowley was perfectly cool about it. 'Do I have your permission?'

There was a perceptible hesitation before the minister nodded. 'Very well. Yes.'

And Cowley smiled.

'Good. I'm glad you agreed – because I've already got Doyle and Bodie up there!'

The scene could have been any new town development. Concrete. Plastic. Glass. A shopping precinct with parallel rows of plate-glass windows, gaudy lettering giving names repeated a thousand times in other shopping precincts and high streets of the country, the superficial glitter and glamour of the consumer society showing off, the scene held little attraction for Doyle and Bodie as their car nosed up to the kerb. This was the world of soap powders, baked beans, refrigerators, packet soups, the world of instant this and that, the empire of special offers and discount stamps and sales every other week. The people moving busily about all seemed to have somewhere to go. Doyle halted the car.

He looked across the road and nodded towards one of the supermarkets, a butterfly's wing of display, the wire trolleys stacked outside.

'There used to be an old cinema there – a flea-pit. I'd put on my dad's coat, turn the collar up, lower my voice . . . Pretend I was eighteen, and get in to see the X movies.'

Bodie nodded sympathetically. 'Your home town, eh?'

'No. Not quite. But we spent a few years here. I was at school here for a while.' He half-shut his eyes. 'It's changed.'

'Everything', said Bodie with immense wisdom, 'does.'

Doyle took no notice. 'Over there – just to the left – there was a dance hall. And a girl called Ann . . . Or was it Annette? Big, tall blonde. She was the first girl I – '

He stopped speaking as a blue shadow moved at the side window and a sharp rap sounded on the roof of the car. The policeman bent down to look in. He was young, smart, pink-cheeked, and he looked perfectly calm and composed.

Bodie said: 'Something wrong?'

'You're parked in a no parking area, sir.' The policeman's voice was perfectly polite.

Bodie felt the petty annoyance wash over him. 'Parked! We were stopped to – '

The policeman interrupted firmly. He did not look quite so young now. 'You're pulled into the kerbside, your wheels have stopped rotating. That's the definition of parking, sir.'

The policeman regarded them levelly. A few tiny drops of sweat clung to his upper lip. 'Of course, if you would rather I gave you a ticket, sir . . . '

Bodie opened his mouth and Doyle, leaning forward, said firmly: 'No, we're moving.'

He put the car in gear and drew away, leaving the not-so-young policeman staring after them, his hand still at his pocket flap.

Staring back, twisted in the seat, Bodie glared venomously.

'The stupid, jumped up – '

114

'We,' interrupted Doyle, 'are here to listen, watch, observe.'

'I don't like arrogant coppers.' As he spoke Bodie turned back, favouring Doyle with a mean look.

That was water off a duck's back to Doyle, the ex-copper. 'You do put people's backs up, you know.'

'What?' said Bodie, and then settled back in the seat. He was smug and the tension went away as he said: 'Because I'm too good-looking?' His smile curved those lips in the familiar heart-throb way.

'Because,' Doyle told his partner, 'you are the only pain in the arse that stands out like a sore thumb.'

Very gently, Bodie chided Doyle. 'Doyle – you mixed your metaphors.'

Doyle smiled and tooled the car around past the concrete curve of road where concrete pots held flowers that were not made of concrete, although they might just as well have been. 'Anyway – we know something already. The best-policed city in the country? Looks like it's true.'

It was true and in Chief Constable Gerry Green's office the hows and whys were being spelled out. Green sat at his desk, forceful, fleshy, formidable. Inspector Chives, facing him, looked at ease, confident, a man assured of himself and of what he was doing in life.

'Now what about this football match on Saturday?' Green stirred the paper on his desk where the Saturday derby was advertised in terms just this side of a challenge to the death. 'If there's trouble like the last time –'

Chives shook his head. 'There's bound to be that, sir. The visiting supporters have a reputation for it. But,' and here Chives's mouth widened in a smile, 'they haven't been in this city before, sir. Different League.'

'The match is being televised. I don't want any accusations of police brutality levelled at my force.'

'That's why I've cut the uniformed men to the bone, sir.' At this Green looked surprised, and Chives went on in his heavy, authoritarian way, very satisfied with himself.

'My boys, my special boys, will be in plain-clothes, sir. You won't be able to tell them from the thugs.'

Sharply, Green cut in with: 'I won't have them generating trouble.'

'Stopping it before it escalates, sir. That's a nice, modern media word, isn't it, sir – escalates?' He leaned forward over the desk. 'They'll be mingling with the crowd, a part of it, and *ready*. Anyone steps out of line, and my boys will have him out of the stadium and into a wagon and away. All very discreet.'

'Hm,' observed Green. 'The courts will be full on Monday, then.'

Slowly, Chives shook his head. On his narrow face his smile looked like the smile of an anteater licking up ants. 'Only if we charge 'em, sir . . . And I wasn't thinking of charging them.' Green looked up sharply. Chives went on smoothly, relishing his own cleverness. 'That would be a waste of my men's time, sir. And public funds. No, sir . . . I thought we'd hold 'em for a while, give them a chance to realise the error of their ways . . . And then we'll release them – outside the city, in the early hours of the morning.'

'In the early hours . . . !'

'Long after the last train's gone. It'll be cold and – if we're lucky – raining . . . And a long hike ahead of them.'

The self-satisfied look on that dark narrow face gave Chives the appearance of a triumphant emperor riding rough-shod over the defeated remnants of the revolution.

'Now that's going to make a lasting impression on them, isn't it, sir . . . ? Probably more effective than any fine a magistrate might impose. They'll know that we – this city – mean business.'

Green pursed his lips, not altogether displeased, but cautious.

'It's – unconventional.'

'It's good sense.'

'Nevertheless, I'm not sure I can officially approve – '

Chives interrupted with his trump card.

'Then, I never told you. Did I, sir?'

Doyle and Bodie checked into a small and not particularly salubrious hotel. It was not, as Bodie remarked in his fierce yet off-hand way 'sleazy'; but it was decidedly almost sleazy. It held that indefinable air of grime in the furnishings and carpets, and yet everything was clean to the touch. There was a greyness to the place and the maze of corridors threading through uneven levels. They found their room and dumped their bags on the beds. The room was drear and with vomit-coloured wallpaper and there was a hand basin but no adjacent bathroom.

'I'm not used to sharing,' declared Bodie, looking about, his upper lip lifting. 'Not with a feller, anyway. And I'm not used to anything less than five star.'

'Not on this job.' Doyle wandered across to stare out of the single window. 'Cowley said a low profile.' Bodie saw the way Doyle stood at the window and joined him. Both men stared out morosely at grey rooftops, a billow of steam rising from a square hole in the buildings, more roofs, the distant view of tower blocks, and taking in the muted roar of traffic.

'Could have been worse,' said Bodie, resigning himself to the rigours of undercover operations. 'Could have been near the railway –'

Even as he spoke a diesel train chuntered into sight from a tunnel to the side and hauled its dirty-topped coaches along a track between brick walls. They hadn't spotted that tunnel or the cutting until the diesel hummed and rumbled into sight. Both men waited, perfectly silently, until the train bumbled its noisy way into the opposite tunnel and disappeared from view. Brown diesel fumes hung on the air.

Bodie lifted his shoulders and let them drop, defeated. He crossed to the bed and flopped out. 'It's a bad dream. Wake me when it's over.'

'It's funny,' said Doyle, abruptly.

'Eh?'

'The desk clerk –'

The woman on the registration desk, not quite slovenly, but almost so, had demanded their names and full addresses for the police checks. The police, she had told the new guests, went through the register once a week, regular. Once a day in some districts of the city.

Bodie said: 'Like Germany or France or somewhere.'

'Certainly not like England.'

The partners looked at each other and, suddenly, like a cold shower, they were very serious.

'D'you think,' Bodie said, 'Cowley *is* on to something?'

'A very well policed city,' quoted Doyle. 'And the crime rate's down by twenty-two per cent.'

'But at what price?'

'Well, we'll find out, shall we? Go out on the town in one of those mean districts – where the cops check the register every day.'

Bodie's interest had perked up at talk of going out on the town, but as Doyle went on he felt deflated.

Doyle continued grimly: 'And we go naked.'

He opened his suitcase and carefully stripped away the lid lining to reveal a hollow space packed with foam. Into this receptacle he placed his handgun and then held out his hand.

With a sigh Bodie produced his own Browning auto. Being Bodie he whipped it out of the shoulder holster as though drawing against Wild Bill Hickock. Doyle took the gun and placed it alongside his own. 'And your ID.'

Both ID cards went into the secret foam-lined compartment.

'Just like Cowley said . . . Not a whisper that CI5 are in the area.'

Doyle closed up the lid lining carefully, smoothed it into innocence, and then snapped the lid shut.

When evening closed in they drifted through that part of the city they expected to be jumping. There was a quietness about the area that, for all the bright neons and the people and the music, deadened responses. The place seemed to be having a good time at half-speed and holding its breath expecting trouble.

They wandered into a club where with only minimal fuss

118

they were admitted as paid-up members, with a strong warning on what to say should the police turn up. They nodded understandingly and moved into the place, looking it over, at the small tables and the bar and the décor and the dim lighting. Doyle's face ridged up.

'Villains.'

'Eh?' said Bodie.

'This place – a hang-out for villains. I can smell 'em a mile away.'

The place was a hard club; that was not in doubt. But –

'Villains maybe,' observed Bodie. 'But not being very villainous.'

A thin, nervous-looking man with a very pale face came in and began talking jerkily to the girl who had warned Bodie and Doyle about the police. The girl was Sally, and she was clearly not too pleased to see the man again. He was Terry, and Sally told him: 'I can't serve you, Terry. They'll close me down, take away my licence if they find you here. They warned me.'

'Just one beer, Sal. For old time's sake? Look, I'm just out after a two-year stretch.'

Watching the two talking, Bodie and Doyle listened without appearing to be in the slightest interested. Eventually Sally served Terry his beer, and they saw the girl, at Terry's pleading, hand across four five pound notes. Terry said he needed the loan to catch a train to leave town, and he was most obviously sincere. He drained his drink, looked about so that his eyes gleamed in the lighting, and then went swiftly to the exit.

The CI5 men exchanged a single look. Then they stood up and followed Terry.

Outside it was early dark, and the lights of the club flickered with a palely erratic glow. Across the way lay a waste-land site where old buildings had been demolished and which was now used as a car park. Terry emerged from the club and started off along the uneven pavement.

He halted as though he'd run into a brick wall.

A police car waited along by the end of the car park,

119

silent, not moving, just sitting there.

Terry spun about and, putting his head down, walked very smartly back and ran headlong into Bodie who had just stepped out of the club's door. Terry rebounded and almost fell over Doyle. His white face shone in the club lighting, and his eyes were wide and staring, frightened.

Casually, Doyle said: 'Heard you were going to the station.'

Terry had nearly jumped out of his skin at the collision. Now he spoke so quickly his voice squeaked.

'Yes, yes. Right away . . . I've got my fare . . . I'm leaving . . .'

Bodie with great charm said: 'Then allow us to give you a lift.'

In the car Terry appeared seized with the dire apprehension that Bodie and Doyle were policemen sent to do him a mischief. When they assured him they were not policemen he immediately jumped to the conclusion that suited them.

'We're thinking of moving in on this town,' said Bodie in his Humphrey Bogart voice.

'Moving in?'

'To set up a little business.'

'That's right,' amplified Doyle in his James Cagney voice. 'Want to know the strength of the law around here. It's worth twenty.'

Terry licked his lips. He was still in a terrible state, hesitating; but he had stamina enough to repeat: 'Twenty?'

'Twenty,' said Bodie. And held out the notes.

Terry reached out, took the four fivers, folded them and stuffed them away as an elephant stuffs away a currant bun. Then, his voice much fortified, he said: 'Forget it.'

As Bodie glared at him, he said: 'You want advice – that's it. Forget it. This town's sewn up tight. Why do you think I'm leaving in such a hurry – because of the cops.'

'And if you don't leave?' Bodie frowned. 'What happens?'

'What happens? I've just done a two-year stretch – that's what happens.'

With the mocking tone of the cop who's heard it all before, Doyle said: 'Oh, I see. You were framed?'

'In solid oak! Mind you, I was lucky – not like Henry or Carson, or poor old Jimmy Flynn. He took the biggest fall.'

'Flynn?' said Bodie. 'Who's Flynn?'

'A man who was going straight. They knew it – we all knew it. But –'

Doyle cut in. 'Where's Flynn now?'

'Doing a life sentence.'

The car rounded a dimly-lit corner and wheeled up to a red-brick entrance, arched, and with old-fashioned lamps spilling a welcome amber gleam across the forecourt. The railway station looked forlorn, like an old-timer waiting for the supply wagon to roll in. The smell of diesel in the air was a sad reminder of days when coal dust and steam flavoured the atmosphere around here.

Terry alighted and continued his warnings. 'Proud of its prison, this city is. Thanks for the lift. Now you go set up somewhere else. You've got no chance here . . .'

He would have repeated his last words, for the emphasis and because of the twenty in his pocket, and he started to say: 'No cha –'

His pale face went taut. His eyes abruptly looked hollow above the white cheekbones.

The police car drove quietly into the forecourt and circled around, lazily, like a shark, and drew up across the way. Terry swallowed.

'I've got to go!'

He turned and fairly bolted into the station through the brick archway. Bodie and Doyle looked after him until he vanished, then they stared at the police car, and then at each other. That dark police car exuded menace.

Chapter Nine

The first reports sent in by his ace operatives caused George
Cowley's sensitive nose for villainy to twitch.

The information on the man Flynn was so hearsay it
would not even be looked at; but nonetheless he called in
the relevant files and went through them. That wonderful
period when the damned bullet in his leg had ceased pain-
ing him appeared to be ending; he had had a couple of
nasty goes and darkly suspected there were more to come.
As far as George Cowley was concerned, the Condor Legion
should have been left out for the vultures. But, the man
Flynn ...

He made the claim to Doyle, who as the ex-copper had
visited the prison, that he had been framed for the murder
of a local hard boy because he had once worked for him.
Flynn's explanation of the box-up had been that 'they don't
like unsolved crimes in this city . . . Anything to keep the
record straight.'

Cowley sipped thoughtfully at a pure malt and when the
doorbell rang he smiled just enough to make the creases
around his mouth soften his whole craggy face. He seldom
smiled like that when his men were around – particularly
those two tearaways, Doyle and Bodie. His flat looked
exactly the same as it had when he'd brought Pellin up

here to open up this whole can of worms. Now he answered the door to the minister, who would – who would have to – go fishing with some of those worms.

The minister looked handsome and distinguished and just a trifle flushed. He wore evening dress and was clearly not fully at ease.

'It's the turn of Mohammed to come to the mountain,' he said by way of starters.

Cowley ushered him in, saw to his hat and coat, offered drinks, sat him down. 'Thank you,' was all he allowed himself by way of comment on the minister's quip.

'Developments?'

'The faintest whiff of something nasty,' Cowley told the minister. 'I want to lean on your brilliant legal record.'

'Long time ago, George.'

'But you can still read between the judicial lines, I hope?'

As the minister glanced up questioningly at Cowley's tone and words, the CI5 chief placed a batch of files tied with green laces on the mahogany side table.

'First,' he said, 'the case of a man named Flynn. Lots of circumstantial evidence. And then,' he tapped the files. 'Half a dozen trial transcripts selected at random. Cases that ended in a conviction for Green's police force.'

The minister looked judicial. 'The Home Secretary wouldn't like that, George.'

As Cowley started to bristle, the minister went on: '*Green*'s police force? You make it sound like a private concern.'

Very grim, very uncompromising, Cowley said: 'Yes.'

'George – ' The tone of pleading admonishment, of surprised despair, in the minister's voice made no impression on Cowley.

'I'm making no accusation,' he said. 'Yet. But Doyle and Bodie are still in that city, checking . . .'

As the evening closed in it seemed the frenzied cheering and roaring, the shouts and yells, the singing ritualistic chants echoed still over the rooftops and chimneys of the city where Doyle and Bodie were, as Cowley had said, still checking. The home team had won. Football was a small part of what had really happened this afternoon in the stadium. Football was merely the excuse. And the visiting team's supporters were in for a rude surprise when – as inevitably they would – they attempted to rid themselves of their baffled and beaten fury. Gerry Green's city would deal with them mercilessly.

Many an outraged shopkeeper surveying his smashed windows, many an inoffensive citizen crudely jostled from the pavement into the gutter, many a landlord of many a pub, welcomed his city's handling of thugs and tearaways and young hooligans. Football was a game. These scum who followed the teams solely for the aggro had made of sport a mockery and a byword for filth and degradation. And when they threw darts – perhaps that lonely little island had the right answer there. The authorities were too soft on football crowd terrorists. Yet Gerry Green's city felt, somehow, that they could welcome the evening and night of celebration, and feel secure.

Very few of them even thought to question how the miracle was achieved. They saw the results and felt civic pride.

Bodie and Doyle, well aware of that civic pride and what it entailed, looked closely at its roots and origins.

Like George Cowley, they had seen authority in action, and they could pick the winners from the losers, the authority that never lost sight of its responsibility and the authority that fed on its own power. This was England, not some banana republic, not some newly-liberated country of the dark continent. CI5 had been established to fight crime on its own terms, and the Big A had established a ferocious reputation for doing just that. But CI5's brief extended also to the abuse of power . . .

At closing time the pubs and clubs were heavily policed.

Bodie and Doyle watched a pub where from the noise and laughter it was fairly to be expected that fireworks would explode. They were not disappointed.

124

On a wave of laughter and the dissipating fumes of alcohol a big man – a large, cheerful, teddy-bear big man – blundered out of the pub with an arm wrapped around the waist of a girl on each side. The three were happy and giggly-laughing, and it was perfectly plain to Bodie and Doyle that the big man, filled with bonhomie, was too far gone to drive. His glowing face sweated his good humour as he looked about.

'It's back to my place – and celebrate some more.' Then the hard, watchful, stony faces of the police swam into his vision. 'Hey, the fuzz in this town take a personal interest, don't they? I like that. I like it.' The big man and the two pretty girls, giggling, moved forward towards the waiting police. ' . . . know how to make a stranger feel at home.' He looked about owlishly. 'Now where's that car of mine?'

He moved on, his meaty hands clasping the waists of the girls. Then he halted, tilting his head over the hair of the girl to his left, smiling craftily at the clustered police.

'Oh, no. I'm not driving. Responsible citizen, I am. So . . . So responsible – I'm going to lock it up.'

He was near enough to the waiting police now as the other customers of the pub streamed past to unwind an arm from the girl to his right. With a fatuous smile of pure affection on his sweating face, the big man prodded the nearest policeman in the chest.

'Lock it up, in case it gets stolen. Wouldn't want to add to the crime rate.'

Like a chariot of the gods descending in golden glory a taxi rounded the corner and bore down towards the pub. The orange light over the screen glowed like the sacred flame. The big man hiccoughed and smiled and raised his arm. 'Taxi!'

The taxi-driver, born like all taxi-drivers with eyes covering every part of his anatomy, swerved towards him. He swayed, laughing, saying: 'Yes, should lock the car and take a taxi.'

The girls were solicitously ushered into the cab by the big man, rather like a bear might stuff honey into a hole in

125

a tree, and, swaying and recovering with enormous dignity, he stepped back.

'Wait here – lock the car. Yes, even with all these lovely coppers about – should lock car.'

Watching this, listening, aware of the sights and sounds and smells of the night and the emptying pub and car fumes Bodie and Doyle saw the big man sway up to a narrow-faced man who was almost as big as the drunk. 'Going to lock my car.'

The plain clothes policeman's face did not change expression. But he turned away and gave a nod to a uniformed policeman at his side.

Casually, the CI5 men sauntered towards the car park through the confusing lights and shadows. The uniformed cop walked with a purpose, following the big drunk.

The car was big, like its owner, an expensive Daimler, lovingly polished and with car-club badges festooning the badge rail. The drunk pulled out his keys and leaned down to the door lock. The uniformed policeman appeared soundlessly at his side.

'Excuse me, sir . . .'

The policeman extended a breathalyser.

'I have reason to believe that you have been drinking and as you are in charge of a car I must ask you to take a breathalyser test.'

The big drunk chuckled happily. He blinked. It was a joke.

'Come on . . .'

The policeman's face remained as stony as a headstone. He pushed the breathalyser forward menacingly.

'Are you refusing to take a test, sir?'

The big smile faded, the brows drew down. The joke was suddenly not funny through all the happy fumes. 'Refusing? Of course I'm damned well refusing. In charge of a car? I'm locking it. That's all. Locking it.'

The narrow-faced plain-clothes man walked towards the Daimler and the big drunk and the uniformed policeman.

Bodie and Doyle, both, could see how the plain-clothes man was enjoying this scene.

'If he refuses the test, you are empowered to arrest him, constable.'

The big man stared. He couldn't really get to grips with what was happening. 'I've got a taxi waiting. *You* know that.' His stare challenged the detective, who remained silent, watchful. 'I told you – just going to lock my car.'

The constable pushed the breathalyser forward. 'Sir – '

With a gesture compounded of petty anger and disbelieving annoyance, the not-so-happy drunk knocked the breathalyser from the policeman's hands.

'What is this?' he demanded, truculent and yet with caution trying to get through the alcohol.

The detective bent, retrieved the breathalyser and held it up. It was broken. He smiled again, and this time there was no mistaking the anticipation in that narrow face.

'Damaging police property. Arrest him, constable.'

The policeman moved forward, ready to obey the orders of his superior. The big man pushed him away, a teddy-bear shove.

At this Inspector Chives' narrow face broke into a feral smile of total pleasure. Now he had the big drunk. He raised his voice.

'Resisting arrest. Assaulting a police officer.' He shouted now towards the other policeman by their cars. 'This officer requires assistance.'

As the reinforcements ran over the constable tried to grab the big drunk again and was shoved off once more for his pains. The other policemen arrived and piled in, and now the big man's face lost all its good humour. He began to resist in real earnest, and the police, nothing loath, piled on the pressure. Chives stepped in. Taking his aim with accuracy, taking his time in the fight, he dodged in and holding his hand very low hit the big man. He hit hard. He hit low. He hit foul.

The big man was shouting now, a policeman's cap spun away, the blue uniforms were piling in, and the big man

127

was going down, yelling, his frenzied face aware at last of what was happening. Chives drew back his fist for a final savage blow.

A voice spoke crisply.

'That's enough, isn't it?'

Chives spun about. He saw Doyle standing there, the lumps in his jaw working, his blue eyes very bright in the pub lights. Doyle went on in a clipped way: 'The minimum amount of force to overcome resistance.' He nodded to the big man who was gasping for air like a stranded fish. 'I don't see him resisting any more.'

The big man folded to his knees. He was hurt. Chives grunted and rapped out: 'Oh, you're some kind of lawyer, are you?'

'I know my rights.'

'Do you? Do you!'

The whole scene was ugly and distasteful to Ray Doyle. He'd tried to be a good copper, and he'd seen some bad ones, and some thoughtless ones, and careless ones. He just didn't like the smell of this little lot, not one little bit at all.

Inspector Chives crossed the space between them with the aggression of a stalking tiger. He stared at Doyle, a hard, intent, devouring stare. Without turning his head, he said: 'Edwards.'

The uniformed policeman reacted to the flat metallic tone. 'Sir.'

'Isn't this the man wanted for that break-in at South Street last Wednesday?'

Police constable Edwards hesitated. The breathalyser test had been ordered and he had tried to carry it out. This man, now . . . He hesitated. Then: 'Looks very much like him, sir.'

'Yes,' said Chives, and that metallic purr of satisfaction thickened in his voice. 'Yes, very like him. I think we should take him in for questioning.'

Doyle said nothing. He recognised all the awful symptoms of what was going on. Chives' triumphant face leered on him. Bodie stepped up. Bodie's mobile lips were firmed and his famous eyebrows were drawn down. He spoke evenly; but the rasp of repressed passion made Doyle raise an eyebrow.

'It's not possible,' said Bodie. As Inspector Chives rounded angrily, Bodie went on: 'Last Wednesday? We weren't even in this town last Wednesday. *And I can prove it.*'

A slight pause ensued in which all that repressed passion in Bodie evaporated, so that he spoke with a winning smile, all placating and jolly-friendly.

'One of those regrettable cases of mistaken identity ... ?'

Chives regarded them slowly, insolently. He was thinking. Then: 'What's your name?' As Doyle hesitated in his turn, Chives rapped out: 'I know *my* rights, too. Loitering in a car park, perhaps with intent to steal. Name?'

'Doyle.'

'And you?'

'Bodie.'

'Address?'

Bodie said: 'We're both staying at the Star Hotel, Beak Street.'

Chives' narrow lips broadened into that rat-trap smile.

'Not from this area, eh?'

The police were half-carrying half-dragging the moaning form of the big man to a patrol car. He had been worked over before Doyle intervened, a quick, efficient and thoroughly nasty job. It had been too quick, far too quick ...

'Fortunately,' said Doyle, the answer remote enough to pass.

Inspector Chives favoured them with a hard scrutiny, the kind of look that stirred hatred, then he walked off towards the cars. Bodie and Doyle stared after him. Hatred like that was a double-edged weapon.

Inspector Chives was a very angry man. The anger and resentment boiled in him. He'd worked damned hard to

9   129

clean up the city with full authority from the chief constable. He took a long slug of scotch straight from the office bottle and bawled: 'Edwards!'

When police constable Edwards was standing in the office, Chives said. 'Those two jokers outside that pub. They're staying at the Star Hotel. They looked at me with dumb insolence, Edwards. I don't like 'em. Either of 'em.' He took another drink and then a deep dragging breath. 'They are not the kind of persons the Chief would want in this city, Edwards.'

Blank faced, Edwards said: 'No, sir.'

'Chivvy 'em, Edwards. You know the drill. If necessary we'll get the special squad to mount an operation. You can handle it.' His big hand gripped the neck of the bottle. 'I keep the city clean. I don't want scum like that fouling the pavements.'

'Yes, sir,' said Edwards, dutifully.

Inspector Chives went along to the chief constable's office with much of that glow of righteous anger hanging about him like a thundercloud. He was well aware that he was a hard man, and his reputation ensured that when he said jump, his men jumped.

Chives liked that.

Gerry Green had just finished Chives's reports when the inspector knocked and entered. The unspoken compact between the two men showed its results in the figures and the statistics.

' . . . control of the football hooligans,' Green spoke half to himself and half to the inspector, riffling the reports. 'Very commendable.'

Chives smiled. 'Said it would work, sir. The word will get around. This isn't a city to take liberties with.'

'Or in.' Green shoved the papers aside. 'Anything else?'

'No. Oh, yes, sir. Couple of undesirables. Villains, I'd say.'

Green looked up and an irritated frown crossed his face. 'Anything solid against them?'

'No, sir. But my instincts tell me they might be trouble.'

'I like instincts, Chives.' Green's heavy face broke into the beginnings of a smile. 'They can't be put on paper.' The smile faded. Green leaned forward and his face ridged into lines of authority. 'Undesirables. I don't want them in my town, inspector.'

Chives's smile was quite unaffected, for the old man was taking perfectly the line Chives had known he would and had already prepared for.

'No, sir.'

The word got around.

Bodie and Doyle were soon picked up driving sedately through the city's busy shopping streets, turning out on to the ring road and running ninety degrees and then rolling back. They were followed from point to point until P.C. Edwards in his patrol car tailed on to them turning into Corporation Street. Department stores and glittering shops passed to either hand, the pavements were crowded, the weather looked to stay fine, and the partners took in the scene with their professional instincts at full alert whilst they chatted seemingly casually.

'Look,' said Bodie at last, always restless. 'I reckon we got enough last night. Their police procedure – '

'Stinks, I know.' Doyle shook his head. 'But we saw only one isolated incident. Could be just one heavy copper . . . '

'And what about Flynn? He was framed.'

'He *says* he was framed.'

Bodie turned to squint at his partner. As he spoke Ray Doyle, for a single instant, couldn't make up his mind if Bodie was putting on the wistful, little-boy-lost look, or if he really felt so deeply the stench of this city. For Bodie's expression was that chin-in, long-faced, reproachful pleading look he could put on so well that devastatingly involved a little pouting tremble to the lower lip.

'Doyle,' said Bodie. 'Let's go home. I like home. I miss it.'

Of course he was putting it on, reasoned Doyle, in that flash of exasperated amusement. Bodie went on mournfully.

'I have near and dear ones at home. And there is one particular redhead – '

'She,' said Doyle, with firmness, 'will keep.'

'If you think so. I was going to give *you* her phone number. Come on, Doyle, what about – ?'

They were interrupted by the wail of a police car siren.

The patrol car eased up alongside, neatly slotting in between the opposite-flowing streams of traffic, and Bodie was signalled into the kerb. He complied, and saw the policeman sitting next to the driver was P.C. Edwards.

The affair wended its dreary little way, with the CI5 men being cautioned for exceeding the speed limit. Bodie had been doing around twenty-nine point five to thirty miles an hour. He was a good enough driver to know at what speed his car was going. Edwards accused him, stony-faced, of travelling between thirty-two and thirty-six. There was the usual production of driving licence and documents and Edwards warned Bodie that he would be reported and might face prosecution.

That was the first.

The next one was a nonsense of driving through a red traffic light when Bodie knew damn well it had been green.

Trouble was, the cop – and it was Edwards again – had his partner in the patrol car and both policemen said they were prepared to swear the light was red.

The partners received another warning.

They were hounded around the city, shaken as a terrier shakes a rat.

They were, in the elegant words of Inspector Chives, chivvied.

When Edwards got them again for failing to stop at a zebra crossing – the black and white and orange-lit safety zone across the road had been empty when Bodie drove across – and again stated he and his mate were prepared to swear that Bodie had almost hit a little old lady with her old-age pension book clutched in her hand, the partners exchanged disgusted looks.

Edwards leaned down to look at them in the car.

'I would drive carefully in future if I were you, sir,' he advised Bodie. 'You see, this is a clean, safe city. We're proud of that. In fact, sir, I would suggest that if you feel unable to measure up to our very high standards, you should leave town, sir.' He straightened up and then, very fast, very menacingly, bent down again to the window.

'As soon as possible,' he said. 'Sir.'

When the Edwards wart had gone Bodie and Doyle sat for a bit. The police car waited on their tail. They knew it would move off when they did. They knew that it would follow them.

Presently, his forefinger and thumb gently rubbing his chin, Doyle said: 'Tell me more about this redhead.'

Bodie perked up instantly.

'Home?'

'Home,' said Doyle. 'Yeah, it's time to go home.'

Doyle and Bodie did not expect to transact their business at Cowley's flat very often. The spartan – a euphemism for shabby and rundown – premises occupied by CI5 H.Q. saw their usual reports and meetings. But Cowley and the minister felt themselves to be walking on soft-boiled eggs on this one. The minister was most concerned and he didn't give a damn that he was showing that concern. He paced irritably about Cowley's flat as Bodie and Doyle watched silently.

'How, George, tell me how? How do I present these facts? I accept what you've told me.' This to Bodie and Doyle. 'You've done an excellent job.' Back to Cowley, he said fretfully: 'But what have they told me? A city sewn up tight – and safely? A city where hooligans are kept in check and suspicious characters forced to move on? For God's sake, George, to most law-abiding citizens it sounds like Utopia!'

'Aye,' said Cowley in his dour way. 'That's what some thought about Hitler's Germany.'

'Green is doing a wonderful job.' The minister made the

133

remark flat and yet insistent. 'The trial transcripts show nothing conclusive –'

'Couldn't agree more on that,' said Cowley. 'If you take each case on its merits, nothing at all. But if you look at them overall they're very heavy on circumstantial evidence, *convenient* circumstantial evidence . . . Stolen goods found in a basement . . . Drugs found in coat pockets . . . Offensive weapons in the boot of a car . . .'

'George – there's nothing substantial, not even now –' The minister stopped pacing and glared. 'And I still say he's doing a good job –'

'Because he's slamming doors on porn and hoodlums and anyone who doesn't measure up to his particular standards? Suppose his standards change? Suppose he clamps down on those who don't go along with *his* politics? Or ethnic groups, or people who grow their hair below the Plimsoll Line . . . Or anyone who, in *his* opinion, doesn't measure up?'

The minister stared at George Cowley and for the umpteenth time reminded himself of the reason for the existence of Cowley's Incorruptibles.

'Unbridled power,' said Cowley, and his craggy face bore no single trace of a smile, of anything yielding as he spoke. 'It's the thing I've been fighting all my life! It starts wars, and it hurts people, and *it's damned bloody dangerous!*'

Bodie and Doyle and the minister waited, frozen, as Cowley's outburst seemed to echo and ring about the room. The silence held. The ticking of the ormolu clock began to make itself heard with the cracking clack of a typewriter. Then:

'I', said George Cowley, 'can go over your head, William. I can. But I don't want to.'

The two men stood facing each other, taut, well aware of the importance of the moment and of the passions seething below the surface. The minister drew a breath. His face sagged.

'Evidence. Bring me facts, George. Something solid. Irrefutable.'

134

The partners glanced at each other, with Bodie's eyebrows doing wonderful aerobatics, and Doyle's face expressing the growing understanding of a beautiful situation to come. The minister took his departure, brisk now and all no-nonsense.

'I can't have you going over my head, George.' He was genial in his briskness. 'Then you'd *really* think you were God!'

When the minister had gone Cowley slowly turned and faced his two operatives. These were the two he called his ace operatives, those he cherished, those who, like all CI5 men, would have to go up to the sharp end and be expendable if the viciousness of the situation demanded it. This was no Blind Run, and Cowley had no expectations of that kind of operation. Spelling it out, he told them what they already knew.

'Irrefutable,' said the chief of CI5, the Big A. 'Meticulous detail. The rules of evidence.'

The partners nodded. It was going to be a lulu.

Pellin's back had stopped actively hurting; but he was still stiff and sore. The branding punishment to his spirit, his sense of self, would last far longer than the bodily punishment. He called Inspector Chives's office and was put through after a delay in which no doubt his name was being remembered.

'Inspector Chives here, can I help you, sir?'

'My name is Pellin. Thomas Pellin. I'm secretary of the Gay Youth Organisation.'

There was a perceptible pause on the line.

'Yes, Mr Pellin,' said Chives at last. 'I recall ...'

'Then you also recall I had some trouble in your city recently?'

This time the pause held a different meaning. Somewhat more brusquely, Chives said: 'What's the problem?'

'I'm going to try again. I'm coming back to reopen a branch of my organisation.'

'I – see ...'

'Well, in view of what happened last time, I'd like some police protection.'

Chives's pause again held a different meaning.

'We'll do our best, sir.'

'Thank you.'

'When do you intend returning, sir?'

'My colleagues should be there on Thursday.'

'And where?'

'I've taken offices at thirty-six Canal Street.'

Just before the line went dead, Chives said again: 'We'll do our best, sir.'

Pellin hung up. He was trembling just a little and a fine sheen of sweat across his forehead caught the lights in Cowley's office. George Cowley reached across and switched off the tape recorder connected to the telephone. The whole conversation now rested magnetically in the tape, and that was something that Inspector Chives did not know.

'Thank you, Mr Pellin,' said Cowley. He turned to Bodie and Doyle who had listened intently throughout. 'So nobody outside of this room knows of Mr Pellin's intentions.'

'Nobody,' said Bodie, in his dry way, 'except *their* police.'

Cowley took off his glasses and swung them by an earpiece. When he spoke he sounded extraordinarily soft and cunning, like a Gunpowder Plotter actually under the Houses of Parliament.

'You get back there,' he told Doyle and Bodie. 'I'll make my way there tomorrow.'

As the partners looked in surprise at him, he let that ferocious smile turn his lips lopsided.

' " Know thine enemy" – one of my favourite cliches. I want to know Gerald Green.'

True to his word George Cowley travelled up, and he went by train, announcing his coming. The chief constable sent a car to the station for him. In Green's office after the polite preliminaries, Green sat back, smugness written all over him as Cowley thanked him for sending the car.

'But the route from the station here to your office?' said

Cowley. 'I suspect the driver came the long way – through the park. On your instructions?'

Green smiled. 'They said I couldn't hide anything from you. Yes, a small conceit. I'm very proud of that park, Mr Cowley. A few years ago, no decent woman could walk there, no honest citizen could –'

Cowley smiled, interrupting. 'I thought the grass needed cutting.'

If there was one thing that was true blue about Gerry Green, he was short on humour. He looked uncertainly at Cowley. Then he chuckled. He chuckled real well. 'The grass? Very good! Very good.'

'You needn't have sent a car. My visit here is quite unofficial and informal.'

'They told me. But old habits die hard, the old courtesies. Esprit de corps?'

Cowley inclined his head. 'Oh, which service were you in?'

Green's fleshy face suddenly looked older and he glanced away.

'None.'

'Oh?'

Green spoke stiffly and, quite clearly to the shrewd eyes of Cowley, he had touched on a sore subject. 'An occasional touch of blood pressure. Kept me out of active service, I'm afraid.'

'Oh, I'm sorry.' Cowley made it sound genuine. 'Still, you've more than compensated for it since then.'

At this Green recovered and beamed, taking Cowley's meaning at face value, quite unaware of the darker implications that were in the forefront of the CI5 chief's mind.

'Ah,' Green smiled. 'Even from up here news travels to London, does it? Yes, I hope so. I hope I have done a good job here.'

'Unique.'

'From you that is high praise. Now, then, will you have a drink?'

137

Cowley brightened up at once, feeling the need for a trifle of inner sustenance. 'Well, a wee drop of – '

Green carried on talking, drowning him.

'Tea? Coffee? We have decaffeinated if you prefer?'

After that social courtesy Gerry Green fancied that they got along splendidly. Like a house on fire, as he said. A meal was provided and something of the offices shown and then Green began to warm for the real reason he felt convinced lay behind the visit of the chief of CI5 to his city.

'I must say, George – you don't mind if I call you George? After all, I feel we *are* close colleagues under the skin.'

'Not at all, Mr Green.'

But Green entirely missed that formal rejoinder, busily leaning forward, looking wise and arch and trying to suppress the bubbling excitement at what he believed was going on.

'George. An informal visit? I know how busy you must be . . .'

'It was inevitable I'd drop by sooner or later. Your force's record of arrests – '

'Not just arrests.' Green spoke with pride born of utter conviction. 'Arrest is impotent without conviction.'

A knock tapped smartly on the door and Inspector Chives entered briskly. He saw Cowley and his narrow face registered the man and his reputation. 'Oh, sorry, sir – '

'No, no, come in Chives.' To Cowley, expansive, beaming, Green said: 'Never stop a good copper working, eh? Chives, this is George Cowley, CI5. Inspector Chives.'

Chives said in his stiff and formal way: 'Sir.'

Green went on: 'The inspector's one of my very best men.'

Chives regarded Cowley. 'Not quite good enough, though.' As Cowley glanced up at this, the inspector continued with more than a trace of bitterness breaking through his words: 'Oh, you probably don't remember, sir, but when you first started CI5 I wrote to you, sir, applied

138

to join. I don't suppose you ever saw my application and records?'

Cowley stirred in the chair. There was something about this inspector, so smart, so tough, that got under his skin.

'Or perhaps I did.'

That waspish remark was clearly too much and as Chives reacted with an abrupt frown Cowley went on smoothly, covering up his lapse.

'We were – still are – a very small unit. And very selective. Not room for every man . . . '

Green saved him further explanation, breaking in to say in his heavy cheerful way: 'Not even the best,' and giving Chives a warm and friendly smile.

Chives pulled his shoulders back a little, perhaps a little doubtfully, and then went on with routine.

'Just a report, sir. On the Gay Youth Organisation.'

Green's face darkened at this, but he retained enough of his geniality to handle it lightly.

'I thought they decided not to set up here?'

'Apparently they've changed their mind, sir. Opening up again. Offices in Canal Street.'

'Well.' Green glanced at Cowley, and shook his shoulders, aware of the CI5 man's interest in the exchange. 'Well, we're not here to judge the foibles of human behaviour. Just make sure they respect my law. I leave it to you, Chives.'

Chives said in his flat voice: 'Yes, sir.'

He understood perfectly what the chief constable meant. He had oiled his leather belt. It was exceedingly supple.

Thirty-six Canal Street had not yet fallen down. Maybe the S-irons in the walls, and the flying buttresses of twelve by twelves helped. There were more than a few slates missing off the roof, and the wood of the windows was down past the primer and showed black and crumbly. The bricks of the walls were shedding the mortar between them that had been rammed in before Queen Victoria went into black clothes. But it was habitable, and here Bodie and Doyle unloaded stacks of leaflets from a small pick-up.

They had checked back into the hotel, with Bodie making snide remarks about how *great* it was to be back.

Doyle had simply flipped the lid of his case open and handed across the CI5 ID cards.

'This time it's different, Bodie. Very different.'

So they stacked the piles of gaudily-printed leaflets on the pavement ready to carry them into the building. The brick walls of the street stretched away to a cross street, and then a police prowl car nosed into view.

The partners went on unloading the pick-up.

The police car turned into the street and rolled gently past number thirty-six. The two cops inside favoured the pick-up and the men stacking leaflets with long hard stares.

The car moved on.

When it passed around the far corner and vanished from view the CI5 agents exchanged a single glance.

'I think,' said Doyle. 'We got a nibble.'

Chapter Ten

The chief constable sat down with a satisfied grunt, hitching his trousers, looking across for the steward. His club was exclusive, redolent of the scents of old leather and cigar smoke and fine wines. George Cowley sat down opposite Green and contemplated his host's possible choice of drinks. He'd once had to suffer the horror of eating a dinner during which the four people at the table had been regaled with half a bottle of wine – between them.

'Well, George,' said Green. 'I've given you the grand tour. What do you think of my city? The air could be sweeter perhaps; but the streets could not be safer.'

'Your city?'

Green looked perplexed, not catching on.

'*Your* city. *Your* law. You take a very personal stand.'

'Paternal pride!' Green's face expressed astonishment and then comprehension. 'Isn't that what's needed these days? A personal morality? We see all around us the continuing decline in standards and yet . . . My city? Yes, I try to put my stamp on it. But, big as it is, it's just a small part of this fine, proud country. A small part I can influence.' He was utterly sincere. Because of that he could expand the idea, and so he went on: 'Oh, but that's nothing compared to you, George, eh? East to West, right across

141

the compass is *your* responsibility. I envy you. Your influence . . . The whole country . . . '

'Envy?' said Cowley. 'The thought of that responsibility doesn't – intimidate you?'

'Intimidate?' Green was stimulated by his thoughts. 'Excites, George, it excites me. To have *everything* in my palm . . . '

He clenched a fist on the table. He looked wrought up, exalted, almost, at the vision in his head. Cowley felt a twinge of – hardly sorrow, not concern, perhaps a twinge of despair at the way sincere motives twist and distort under pressure.

'Well,' he said diplomatically, 'that is something we should talk about. Sometime. Later. Now – you mentioned dinner?'

Something sparked in Gerry Green, something Cowley had said, some impression the CI5 chief had given. Cowley wanted his dinner. Whatever it was Green thought he had seen, it might go away after a good meal.

At the Canal Street offices Bodie and Doyle had finished unloading the leaflets and now they prepared to receive the visit they confidently expected. The leaflets were still bundled up; but Bodie had glanced through a few of them with suitable Bodie-type comments.

'Cooking on a budget,' he said, smiling. 'Post natal depression.'

'That's right. Not a single poster, not one word about Gay Youth.'

'That's a relief. My image remains untarnished.' Bodie hauled up another tract and chuckled, pleased. 'Hey,' he said, flapping the paper. 'Mouth to mouth resuscitation.'

When the two cars pulled quietly into the kerb and Chives with Sergeant Reed and his men entered, the office was empty. The special squad wore their stocking masks. They looked about and Sergeant Reed said in a disgusted voice: 'Nobody here.'

'Haven't moved in yet, then,' Chives said. 'Never mind. You can come back tomorrow.'

They returned to their cars and drove off and Bodie and Doyle left their place of concealment in the inner room. The S.L.R. camera with the 2.8 lens clunked and clunked again. The shots were good, black and white, 400 A.S.A film. The car number plates were recorded. Later, when they were developed Doyle checked them out with CI5. He put the phone down, smiling, and turned to the recumbent Bodie.

'Exhibit for the prosecution A.' He lifted one photo. 'One Hillman Hunter, registered to the C.I.D. of this city. And, Exhibit B, one Ford Fiesta, personally registered to Chives, Detective Inspector.'

Bodie lay on the mattress in the back room, eyes closed, hands under his head. A beatific smile played about Bodie's lips.

'Bodie!' Doyle waved the photos under his partner's nose. 'We're on our way.'

Bodie opened his eyes. 'I was dreaming. There were these seven girls, and I was dreaming –'

'The impossible dream!'

Bodie sat up. 'Nothing's impossible. I was very good at maths.'

The look Doyle gave him was, in its own way, remarkable. 'Well, go on dreaming. You need the rest. Because I've a feeling that tonight's the night.'

Gerry Green felt the need to keep up appearances before this important man from CI5, and so he invited Cowley out to his house for the afternoon. The house, of red brick, bowered in greenery and with a fine rose-garden, situated on the outskirts of town in one of the most salubrious quarters, exuded a calm and ordered air. Here a tough no-nonsense man of action could relax and recuperate for the fights ahead.

Green's two teen-aged daughters were laughingly playing with a tethered tennis ball, swatting it backwards and

143

forwards around the post, and Gerry Green, not to be out-done, sweated and lunged and swung his racquet along with them. They made a happy, pleasant, comfortable scene.

Looking on, Cowley felt his eyes puckering in, as though he stared out over a scorching desert under a blinding sun towards the cool beauty of spired minarets and greenly-glowing domes. Gerry Green threw down his racquet and, wiping his neck and face with a towel, came over to Cowley.

'Kids,' he said, glowing with the exercise.

'Two very pretty girls.'

'Yes, and they wear me out.' Green looked at the girls, trim in white, laughing and swatting the tennis ball, laughing as much at the misses as the hits. 'And I love them.'

'Yes. I know you do.'

Cowley's tone caused Green to hold the towel steady by his face, and to look at Cowley in perplexity. But Cowley paced away across the lawn, pensive, his head tilted so that Green could not see his face in the shadow.

'Remember those old films, Green, when we were both kids? The goodies wore white hats and the baddies wore black. Never a grey – not once a grey. They didn't really prepare us for what life is really about, did they?'

Green was openly puzzled. 'I don't understand – '

Cowley hunched himself up and turned to face the chief constable. He tried to find a lighter tone. 'If you had my job, Green, where would you start?'

'Start?'

'Aye. When you took over this city you were a new broom. What about my job? Where would you start sweep-ing?'

As he spoke Cowley walked slowly back, aware of the excitement fizzing in Green. As the chief constable spoke Cowley realised with a stab of comical dismay that this was that special something he had spotted, that the chief constable had got it all wrong, and was wrought up to a fever pitch. For Green prattled on unheedingly: 'I was right. wasn't I, George? Nobody would want to see you go, but the pressures take their toll, and I *am* younger than you, I have proved my worth. This isn't an unofficial visit, is it?'

Cowley simply stared.

'No,' prattled on Green. 'No, I wouldn't expect you to tell me. How could you . . . ? But I've been aware of – of being watched.' He was growing visibly more excited every second. 'If I had *your* job? I – I'd take your lead, maybe tighten up. I think, and I hope you don't mind my saying so, I think sometimes you tolerate too much informality – and I also think you don't always use all the powers of your department to the full. You can cut through the red tape, George. You don't always have to do what is *officially* right – but *right as you see it*. Right as *I* see it.'

He paused, staring at Cowley, all the fizzing excitement tensing him up, taking years off him. Then he shook his head, a little gesture of tacit understanding.

'Oh, I expect there are others in line. Must be. But you *are* here to watch me, George?'

All George Cowley would say was. 'Aye.'

The leaflets in the bundle on the table provided a means of claiming for Post War Credits. The bundle was expertly tied with sisal, and it curved neatly around the Browning auto stuffed into the middle. The butt barely showed. Seated at the table and toying with advice to pregnant ladies conveyed in a tastefully-printed leaflet, Bodie listened to the furtive sounds outside the door that followed the closing of car doors.

The door was kicked open with sudden and brutish power.

Masked men boiled into the office.

Bodie looked up, the startled expression of his face artfully contrived.

Sergeant Reed, his nose and cheeks squashed in by the stocking mask, barged across to the table. 'Hello, darling,' he said, and reached out for Bodie.

With a flair for acting that could have brought him a steady job at the end of the pier, Bodie leaped up and made a frantic dive for the other door. The masked policemen caught and held him easily. He made no resistance.

'Last time your mob moved into our town, they were warned. But not severely enough it seems.' The men turned Bodie around. 'We'll just have to warn you all over again,' said Sergeant Reed. 'Won't we?'

Bodie's shirt went rip-rip down his back. Reed produced a short handled cat o' nine tails from under his coat. The thing was black and obscene, and he flicked it negligently.

He swung his arm back and let his muscles shake out the nine knotted strands. His face expressed a squashed anticipation through the nylon, a grotesque frog-like bloating of enjoyment. He lifted his arm.

A brilliant blue-white flash scythed through the room.

Everyone except Bodie whirled. Through a hole cut in a cupboard door protruded the lens of a camera. As the masked men, caught in a stasis of surprise, froze, the cupboard door swung open. Doyle stepped out. In his right fist he held a gun, and in his left his ID.

'Doyle. CI5.'

Bodie broke the limp grips on his arm without force. He reached and jerked at the bundle, and his gun was in his fist.

Doyle said: 'Bodie.'

'Also,' said Bodie. 'CI5.'

'Let's see their faces.'

'Pleasure,' said Bodie.

The threat of the guns held the masked men. Bodie pushed his gun forward and, reaching out a long arm, ripped the stocking mask off the leader's face. The partners studied the man for a moment, thinking nasty thoughts, and then they ordered the rest of the masks off. Doyle retrieved the camera as Bodie covered the angry, alarmed, crestfallen policemen.

'That's nice. Now – watch the birdie.'

The camera stored away the faces on film.

'Now,' ordered Bodie. 'Turn around. Hands against the wall.' Sullenly, the men obeyed as Bodie said with an

146

infectious humour that chilled them with its menace. 'And let's find out just who you are.'

The wallet came out and was flipped open. Bodie's eyebrows drew down.

'Well, well. Detective Sergeant Reed, of the local constabulary.' He pulled wallet after wallet, and read out the ranks and names. The wallets were tossed on to the table, a mounting pile of condemning evidence. 'What a surprise,' said Bodie, his voice mocking, sarcastic. 'They're all coppers.'

Doyle grabbed Reed's shoulder, spun him about. 'Who set this up? Who ordered this?'

Reed blinked his eyes. He swallowed. He flicked a quick warning glance at his men, a threat. He spoke up boldly enough, still bluff with fancied security.

'No one. We – ' The story came to him. 'We had a few drinks. Then thought we'd have a bit of fun – '

Doyle picked up the discarded cat o' nine tails and swished it. It made a heavy hissing sound. 'Fun!'

'It was no one's idea . . . It just happened . . . We were off duty and – '

Doyle cut in. 'Off duty?' His round cheerful face with that ominous bruise under the right eye tautened. He moved to the table, extricated Reed's wallet, and dialled out on the phone, using the information in the wallet to get through to Reed's local K Division.

'K Division?' He said when he was connected. 'I've some information for Sergeant Reed. Is he on duty?'

The voice on the phone said: 'Yes – but he's out on a special assignment.'

Doyle checked that the tape recorder with its connection to the phone was still running as he said: 'Well, what about Constable Turner?'

'He's on the same assignment as Reed. Can I take a message? Who is this?'

Doyle hung up. He switched off the tape recorder. He looked at Sergeant Reed.

'We'll check the others, for the record.' His look flayed

147

the sergeant. 'But it's going to be the same, isn't it? On duty ... special assignment?'

Sergeant Reed licked his lips. These two men from CI5 exuded an air of total crushing authority that made him sweat.

'Look, we –'

Bodie interrupted. He spoke with distaste.

'All right. You can go.'

'Go?'

'We're tired of looking at you.' Bodie jerked a thumb at the wallets and the tape recorder. 'We've got all we need. Get out of here.'

The men made Bodie feel dirty, and God knew what Ray Doyle the ex-copper was thinking. He gave the sergeant a shove. 'You heard.'

Dazed at the unmasking of their activities and beginning to shudder at what might happen to them, bewildered and apprehensive, the policemen began to drift towards the door.

Toughly, Doyle called after them. 'But you'll be hearing from us.'

The men went out. The room was suddenly full of air, fresher. The inoffensive leaflets lay on the table. The telephone and the tape recorder gleamed under the fly-blown bulb. The dust glittered. Bodie took a deep breath and looked at Doyle. But Ray Doyle, who had tried to be a good copper, pushed his gun away, and did not meet his partner's eyes.

The active mind behind the narrow face of Detective Inspector Chives summed up the situation instantly. Sergeant Reed looked most unhappy as he reported in to Chives in the office; but the inspector had always had the hunch that one day the balloon would go up, But, not in his worst dreams had he envisaged it going quite like this.

'CI5!' he said, and he did not like the sound of his own voice.

'We're done,' said Reed, vaguely. 'Finished.'

'CI5,' repeated Chives. Then: 'They got pictures – ?'

'They got everything. We're sunk.'

'No.' Chives was a man who would fight until the end. 'No – they've got evidence backed by *their* testimony. But they won't present it here, will they? They'll leave town, take it to CI5 H.Q.' He stared calculatingly at Reed, challenging him. He spoke softly, meaningfully, and every word fell distinctly like a pebble into the deepest well in the world. 'But suppose they never leave town?'

Sergeant Reed's face betrayed his own turmoil of emotions. He checked on a half-caught breath, his eyes wide.

Chives went on toughly, ruthlessly, logically. 'You want a few years in prison, sergeant? You know what they do to our kind in prison!' A thought struck him. 'The phones! If they decide to call in ...'

In a welter of activity Chives snatched up the phone and fairly barked his orders.

'Get me the Security Chief of the main switchboard.' To Reed he went on as he waited: 'That's it. We'll handle it as a security operation. A.P.B. all units. Be on the lookout for two men masquerading as CI5 agents. They are armed and dangerous. Issue handguns ...'

Reed protested, incredulous. 'It won't work. This was a planned operation –'

'There'll be a stink, I know. But without those two to back it up ... ? We'll have to resign, yes. But we won't end up in a prison cell.'

'Suppose they've already –'

'We'll attend to the fine details later.' Chives saw it all opening up and he was confident he could pull this one off. It was his neck. 'First thing is to sew up this city and find 'em!' As his connection was made he rapped into the phone. 'Ah, yes, Inspector Chives here. We have a security emergency on our hands and I need your co-operation.'

Sergeant Reed stared at his superior. Drastic diseases required drastic remedies. If they could just get the evidence back ... Reed sensed that Inspector Chives was prepared to go a long, long way to save his neck. Dimly, Reed saw that Chives might be prepared to go all the way . . .

The two CI5 operatives had done their job; but they did not feel they could take very much satisfaction from it. This messy business sickened them. They packed the damning evidence of the wallets and the tape away into a briefcase together with the photographs and then Doyle snapped the locks and said: 'That's it.'

'Better check in and tell them we're on our way.'

Doyle nodded and reached for the phone as Bodie went across to the window, fretting, anxious to be gone from this super-clean and super-corrupt city.

The operator's voice over the phone said: 'All lines to London are engaged. Please replace your receiver and try again later.'

Doyle thumped the receiver back. Bodie sniffed and looked idly through the window. A dark car slid to a halt at the kerb opposite. After a couple of minutes Doyle tried again and again was told all the lines to London were engaged.

Bodie said: 'Doyle . . .'

The tone of his voice made Doyle look up sharply, the phone still clutched in his fist and his face wearing a disgusted look. He slammed the phone down and crossed to the window. Policemen were alighting from the halted car. One of them reached in under his coat and pulled out a revolver. He spun the cylinder, checking for the last time that each chamber was loaded. Satisfied, he joined his partner and started for the shop.

Doyle's round face contracted into a knot of fury.

'Move!'

Bodie and Doyle, snatching up the vital briefcase, dashed for the rear exit.

They bolted out of the back door just in time and hared up a narrow alley. At the end they angled across to another of the tired old grey-brick buildings and eased up to the corner. Bodie put his head around to see a police car just pulling up. A policeman jumped out and as he landed he drew a gun. Bodie hauled back and pulled Doyle with him. They started running the other way. This was one hell of a mess!

They ran quickly towards a narrow alley-mouth that looked invitingly shadowy. Rusty irons protruded from the walls and the rows of windows closed against the air by more wood than glass gave a mouldy look to the buildings. The alley debouched on to another street and a police car speeded along this. The CI5 agents skidded on the stones, backpedalling, frantically dashing diagonally across the street for the sanctuary of the opposite alley.

The police car's siren began to ululate and the tyres screeched as it skidded to a halt. The driver bashed his door open as his partner rattled off the sighting report into the radio.

'Charley Victor Three. We are in pursuit of subjects along Cannon's Way . . . '

Bodie and Doyle raced from the alley and looked about for the next place to hide.

Police constable Edwards heard the report come crackling over the radio and realised he was in a good position to intercept. He started his car and rolled out along the dingy street, feeling the height of the buildings, seeing the slate roofs overtopped by the old brewery that had once disseminated its unique smells over the city.

'Charley Victor Five,' he said. 'On my way to intercept.'

He set the siren screaming and whirled along the street. The brewery vanished beyond a nearer warehouse and then, as Edwards swung skidding around the end of the warehouse, re-appeared. It bulked huge and forlorn, like a stranded dinosaur on a prehistoric beach. Tall chimneys from which no smoke would ever lift again cut thin fingers of blackness against the sky. The grimy walls reared, pockmarked with windows. Other police cars drew up and soon a sizeable force gathered. Edwards reported in.

'Charley Victor Five to Control. The Old Brewery, Venton Street.' More police cars pulled in. 'Suspects believed within the area. If they are, we have them trapped.'

Inspector Chives' heavy voice crackled from the radio. 'This is Chives. Keep 'em pinned down. I'm on my way.' Guns drawn, the police began to approach – warily.

Within the old brewery and huddling in the shadows, Bodie and Doyle could look along the spider-webbed and shadow haunted alleyways where once men had brewed the strong stuff, and see silhouetted against the outside light the ominous forms of police cars and of policemen closing in.

Bodie hefted his gun. His face looked savage.

'We could break out.'

'I know we could.' Doyle's voice crackled with strain. 'And what – take a couple of good coppers with us?'

Bodie looked at him. '*Good* coppers?'

'There's got to be some *good* coppers out there.' Doyle believed that. Anything else would make it all too much of a mockery. 'Out there – following orders – doing what they're told. An army's only as good as its officers.'

They peered through the shadows. The dark and ominous forms were closing in. Doyle said: 'There's a lot of them.' He stood up, suddenly, taking a breath. 'A lot of witnesses.'

He swung the briefcase high and pushed it into the dark crevice between crumbling brickwork. Dust puffed and crumbs of mortar dribbled down. Doyle's face was set.

'What're you doing?'

Doyle brushed his hands together.

'Getting ready to give myself up!'

Bodie gaped at him.

Constable Edwards had returned to his car to report in a so far unwelcome report. The wanted men had not been spotted. Inspector Chives was on his way, and by his voice he sounded to be in the mother and father of a temper. Edwards half turned away from the car and saw a gun, a blue-black automatic, snout into his view. He stiffened in shock. His own gun was pointing in the general direction of Australia.

Then the Browning auto was placed quietly on the

bonnet of the police car and Doyle stepped forward, taking his hand from the gun, and giving a faint, shadowed smile.

'We've had enough,' he said, in a voice that held level, and, somehow, sounded cold and distant.

Edwards recovered from his shock with commendable swiftness. He jerked his revolver up. Bodie stepped up and deposited his weapon alongside Doyle's.

Edwards swallowed and then, feeling relief, shouted.

'Here! Over here!'

Efficiently the partners were placed in the position against the car, hands up, feet out, and their IDs were whipped out. Edwards studied them, frowning.

'They're good. Like the real thing.'

Bodie said: 'They *are* the real thing.'

Edwards' orders said these two were dangerous men masquerading as CI5 agents. He did not doubt his orders.

''Cuff 'em,' he said, and looked up to see Inspector Chives driving up in a dark blue Triumph he'd snatched from the station carpark, so great had been his hurry to get here. Chives strode across, blazing with triumph.

'Who got them?'

'Me, sir,' said Edwards, and felt the pleasure in him at being able to say that.

Chives went over and picked up the two Brownings.

'They were armed, eh?'

'Yes, but – but they gave themselves up.' Edwards was not likely to forget the jolt he'd had when the gun snouted into view. He remembered chivvying these two. Well, it all came to him who waited . . . 'You want me to take them to the main station –'

'No. My car. *I'm* taking them in.'

The police appeared to see nothing extraordinary in this. But Bodie reacted furiously. His face showed his anger as he shouted. 'Now hold on! You're not leaving us with him!'

Chives flicked his hand in irritation towards his Triumph. 'My car . . .'

The police hustled the CI5 men away. As they went

Bodie hollered over his shoulder: 'Those IDs are genuine. Genuine!'

Inspector Chives looked narrowly at Constable Edwards. He was not too happy at what he saw in the young man's face. Smoothly, with great authority, he took the two IDs from Edwards.

'This all they have on them?'

'Those – and the guns –'

'Nothing else? No – bag – of any kind?'

'No, sir. But, sir, don't you think we should –'

Chives gave the constable no chance to make any more of the situation. He interrupted brusquely, turning to march off with his swagger to his car.

'You did well, Edwards.'

As the Triumph started up with the two handcuffed men and Chives, Edwards looked after it. A tiny frown dinted in between his eyebrows.

With Inspector Chives at the wheel, the dark blue Triumph sped out of the city. The houses alongside the road gave way to open fields and trees, with the marching skeletons of the power line pylons bisecting the land. They purred alongside a railway yard for a space and then the road swung left-handed and Chives took the car away up a narrower, rutted track climbing the shoulder of a hill. The clouds lifted high away beyond the city. The car bumped on over the rutted and unmade-up track towards the brow of the hill.

Doyle said: 'You've got to be crazy.'

Perfectly composed, perfectly matter-of-fact, Chives answered. He did not turn his head.

'Yes. I considered that as one line of defence.'

The car jounced on the springs and Chives swung it around for the last curve to the top of the hill. Below on the reverse slope stretched a long smear of rubbish. The tip held the detritus of a city. The Triumph halted facing the drop where the dustcarts reversed cautiously up during working hours, their engines revving noisily, and the backs gaping to spill the waste of the affluent society.

There was not a soul in sight. The noise of a car reached them from the road at the junction where they had left it; but the car itself was out of sight. The smell was a curious one, compounded of rubbish and green growing things. The two mingled inextricably here.

Chives got out and went to the rear door and looked in. His narrow face showed beads of sweat. He spoke directly to Bodie.

'Where'd you plant them?'

Bodie's stare firmed down, hard and unyielding.

'Recordings, photos, come on . . . Where did you leave 'em? Where?'

Bodie said: 'Go to Hell!'

'Where?'

At the silence that was all he got for his answer a red bomb exploded in Chives' brain. He punched Bodie in the face. The punch was unexpected. Bodie tried to move back and Chives hit him again. Blood flecked Bodie's lip. Chives cocked his fist to drive in a third punch and then, with the irrationality fighting his sanity, he paused. He looked cunning, an expression that sickened Bodie and Doyle afresh.

'It doesn't matter,' said Chives. His voice quivered with a passionate conviction. The sweat glittered on his forehead. 'We know where you went. My boys'll find it.'

He slammed the door shut on Bodie, whose lip now bled down his chin. With that swaggering walk emphasised as though he was drunk, he went to the driver's door and, opened it, reached in to start the engine.

Fighting the emotions in himself that wanted him to take off and not stop running, Doyle ground out: 'What did we do? Skid off the road and have a fatal crash?'

The silence all about hung like a shroud.

Chives looked back over his shoulder, his narrow face alive with malicious pleasure at his own cleverness.

'That's the idea. I was miraculously thrown clear.'

Doyle licked his lips. Talk, he had to talk . . .

'And just what were we doing on this road?'

Chives wished to waste no more time. He knew what he was going to do and he intended to do it and he intended to make it look good. He had enough experience, for God's sake!

'You told me about the stuff you'd planted out here.' He switched on and reached for the gear lever. 'I'm a good copper, I had to check, didn't I?'

Aware of the drop below, of what would happen when the car went over that and pitched and rolled and tumbled to the bottom, of the explosion and the fireball, Bodie felt his guts already on fire. With a vicious anger he said: 'A good copper!'

The gear lever was hard and shiny and Chives gripped the knob and started to thrust it forward. In mere heart-beats now the car would roll, and drop, and tumble, and explode...

The CI5 men, handcuffed, writhed to get free, to try to open the door, to do something, anything, to get away. But the car doors were shut. And Chives was thrusting the gear lever home...

A hard, clear, metallic voice said: 'Step away from the car, please, sir.'

Chives spun as though a wasp had stung his rear. His narrow face showed shock. Police constable Edwards had walked silently up the slope of the hill and now he stood, four square, his revolver pointing at the inspector. Edwards' young face showed a grim resolve, and Bodie and Doyle, looking at him, felt their hearts re-entering from orbit.

'You bloody fool!' shouted Chives. 'Get away from here! Forget what you've seen ... !'

Edwards moved forward. The revolver did not waver.

'I'm *ordering* you!' snarled Chives.

Edwards shook his head. The sun caught the metal buttons and insignia on his blue uniform.

'Roust a villain,' said Edwards. He spoke huskily, screwing himself up to doing what he knew he had to do and seeing many things much more clearly than he had for a very long time. 'Lean on him . . . You can order me to do that. Chivvy a hard man, use muscle on the scum, I'll do that . . . But I'm not standing by and watching you commit murder.'

The words were out, spoken, hanging on the air.

Chives glared at the young policeman. A muscle under his narrow cheek bone jumped. Bodie and Doyle felt, both of them, the suspense washing away, the tension relaxing. They had come very near to death, too bloody near . . . The world might not mourn their passing, but they would, both of them, one for the other and for themselves.

Doyle's round face relaxed from that pantherish look compounded of disgust and fear and anger. 'A good copper,' said Ray Doyle. 'I told you. There's always one.'

Edwards held his revolver centred on Chives and the inspector looked with new eyes at the constable. He drew a breath and swung himself around bodily to face Bodie and Doyle in the back of the car.

'It was Green,' said Chives. He spoke with a catch in his breath, a rasp of nerves. 'It was his idea.'

Doyle said: 'Save it for the judge.'

Bodie said: 'But remember what you said.'

George Cowley had begun CI5, the Squad, the Big A, with the express intention of fighting crime on its own terms. He had found crime in many unlikely places. His men had turned over this city and he had found what lurked under the nice clean concrete. He neither much looked forward to nor much regretted the interview with Chief Constable Gerry Green, O.B.E.

Green looked crushed. He sat at his desk and his big fleshy frame was sunken in on the bones, his face grey-green, furrowed, the light gone from the eyes.

'It – it was Chives. He took it upon himself . . . Over-stepped his authority . . .'

Cowley stood, chunky, tough, craggy, and if he stood more on one leg than the other then those who did not know him would not realise he was feeling the most devilish pains from that infernal bullet. But, for this, he did not intend to sit down.

'Chives was a runaway truck, careering down hill, running over the guilty and the innocent.' His plummy voice ground remorselessly on. 'A runaway truck – but you released the handbrake.'

Green said, and he was nakedly pleading: 'George – '

Cowley said in his icy tone: 'The name is Cowley. Mister Cowley.'

He stared at the stricken man, and his face did not soften, could not soften. He knew how to be soft, when he had to be; but other people were involved, other lives, other emotions. He went on speaking and the words were an indictment.

'I don't know what we'll be able to make stick against you, Green. But I *do* know that, whatever the outcome, you'll never again have authority – not even to see kids across the road.'

'My motives, what I did – ' Green looked up, peering through his misery at his nemesis, seeking still to salvage something, trying to find the right words to put what he so clearly saw in his mind, what so many people would now so cruelly misinterpret.

Looking steadily at him, Cowley sensed something of that, saw that the man sincerely believed what he had been doing was the right way. Cowley broke the rules, broke them knowingly and ruthlessly; but he broke the bad rules. And if he didn't have to do that, he would be a happier man. But Green had become obsessed. As he looked, so Cowley felt a shiver of feverish inward fear shudder through him. If ever this was an example of the slave at the back of the quadriga, then he would recognise it and not forget.

Green stared up. His face sagged and his hands shook.

'What I did,' he said. 'I thought it was in the public interest.'

'Aye,' said the chief of CI5. 'That's the tragedy.'

The shopping precinct looked just the same. The same concrete, the same plate glass, the same plastic. The blaring signs were the same. The people looked the same. Doyle and Bodie waited for a while in the car, taking a last look at the scenes of past troubles and past triumphs. The city would go on, rich with life, and the age-old passions of humankind would flower and fester. Perhaps a villain or two might get away with it; but the ordinary folk could breathe easier, even if they did not know it, for Chives and Green, for all their intentions, were the maggots that bred evil.

Bodie sighed and then with one of his cheerful, impish smiles, said: 'They should put up a plaque.'

Doyle favoured him with a glance that was puzzled, for they had done a job, almost got themselves killed, and had managed to come out smelling of violets. As soon as they got back to London and CI5 H.Q. it was a sure bet that Cowley would find them another spot of Mayhem to sort out.

Then Bodie went on in his seraphic way: 'A plaque where you and that blonde got it together.' His voice became mock sonorous: ' "Here, for the first time, Raymond Doyle –" '

Spluttering his indignation, Doyle broke in heatedly.

'First time! First time! Listen – I was nearly fifteen!'

Bodie's pleased smile made Doyle's own smile flash out like the sun from cloud. He started the car and they rolled out, passing the shopping precinct and the concrete tubs with their bright flowers.

'I keep saying it,' said Doyle. 'But this time it's for keeps . . .'

' . . . Let's get out of this lousy city,' Bodie finished.

The car rolled away, back to CI5 H.Q. in London, back to the job, and back to George Cowley.

A selection of bestsellers from SPHERE

Fiction

THE DEATH FREAK	John Luckless	95p ☐
BEL RIA	Sheila Burnford	95p ☐
WOLFSBANE	Craig Thomas	£1.25p ☐
GOODBYE	W. H. Manville	£1.25p ☐
GOLDEN MOMENTS	Danielle Steel	£1.25p ☐

Film and TV Tie-Ins

THE PROFESSIONALS 5: BLIND RUN	Ken Blake	85p ☐
THE PROFESSIONALS 6: FALL GIRL	Ken Blake	85p ☐
THE MUSIC MACHINE	Bill Stoddart	95p ☐
THE PROMISE	Danielle Steel	95p ☐
BUCK ROGERS IN THE 25TH CENTURY	Addison E. Steele	95p ☐
BUCK ROGERS 2: THAT MAN ON BETA	Addison E. Steele	95p ☐

Non-Fiction

THE THIRD WORLD WAR	General Sir John Hackett	£1.75p ☐
INSIDE THE FOURTH REICH	Eric Erdstein	95p ☐
THE CONVICT	Felix Milani	£1.25p ☐
COME WIND OR WEATHER	Clare Francis	95p ☐

All Sphere books are available at your local bookshop or newsagent, or can be ordered direct from the publisher. Just tick the titles you want and fill in the form below.

Name ....

Address ....

....

Write to Sphere Books, Cash Sales Department, P.O. Box 11, Falmouth, Cornwall TR10 9EN.

Please enclose cheque or postal order to the value of the cover price plus:

UK: 25p for the first book plus 10p per copy for each additional book ordered to a maximum charge of £1.05.

OVERSEAS: 40p for the first book and 12p for each additional book.

B.F.P.O. and EIRE: 25p for the first book plus 10p per copy for the next 8 books, thereafter 5p per book.

Sphere Books reserve the right to show new retail prices on covers which may differ from those previously advertised in the text or elsewhere, and to increase postal rates in accordance with the GPO.